JOAN WEIR

Joan Weir is a well-known writer and broadcaster
of young adult fiction. She is the author of more
than six books, including *Balloon Race Mystery,
Career Girl, Secret at Westwind, Ski Lodge Mystery, So,
I'm Different,* and *Storm Rider.*

She is an English instructor at Caribou College
in Kamloops, British Columbia.

CANADIAN TITLES FROM GENERAL PAPERBACKS

Picture Books, Ages 4 - 6

The Picnic	Kady Macdonald Denton	340-494352
Twelve Dancing Princesses	Janet Lunn & Lazlo Gal	458-985406

Fiction & Non-Fiction, Ages 7 - 9

David Suzuki Asks: Did You Know About Light & Sight	Peter Cook & Laura Suzuki	7736-72451
David Suzuki Asks: Did You Know About Insides & Outsides	Peter Cook & Laura Suzuki	7736-72877
The Lady of Strawberries	Helen Chetin & Anita Kunz	7725-90133
Beckoning Lights	Monica Hughes	7736-7280X
Gold Fever Trail	Monica Hughes	7736-72796
Treasure of the Long Sault	Monica Hughes	7736-7277X
A Very Small Rebellion	Jan Truss	7736-72788

Fiction, Ages 9 - 11

Not Impossible Summer	Sue Ann Alderson	7736-72869
Old Coach Road	Wilma Alexander	7736-73059
Queen's Silver	Wilma Alexander	7736-72850
Stampede	Mary Blakeslee	7172-25801
Mysterious Mr. Moon	Anne Stephenson	7736-72842
Lost Treasure of Casa Loma	Eric Wilson	7736-7165X
Terror in Winnipeg	Eric Wilson	7736-71641

Young Adult, Ages 12 & Up

Chapter One	Sue Ann Alderson	7736-72834
Absolutely Invincible!	William Bell	7736-72915
Crabbe	William Bell	7736-7232X
Brothers and Strangers	Marilyn Halvorson	7737-53699
Dare	Marilyn Halvorson	7736-72672
Dreamspeaker	Cam Hubert	7736-72303
Dream Catcher	Monica Hughes	416-052029
Ghost Dance Caper	Monica Hughes	458-802409
Hunter in the Dark	Monica Hughes	7736-72273
Sandwriter	Monica Hughes	416-955207
Far From Shore	Kevin Major	7737-54288
Hold Fast	Kevin Major	7737-54296
Sixteen is Spelled O - U - C - H	Joan Weir	7736-72907

Sixteen is Spelled O-U-C-H
JOAN WEIR

Stoddart

A GEMINI BOOK

Published in 1995 by
Stoddart Publishing Co. Limited
34 Lesmill Road
Toronto, Canada
M3B 2T6

General Paperbacks Edition published in 1991

First published in 1988
by Stoddart Publishing Co. Limited

Canadian Cataloguing in Publication Data

Weir, Joan, 1928–
Sixteen is spelled o- u- c- h

ISBN 0-7736-7290-7

I.   Title
PS8595.E57S5 1991   jC813´.54   C90-095858-8
PZ7.W43Si 1991

Cover Design: David Montle
Cover Illustration: Janet Wilson

Printed and bound in the United States of America

For Michael and Jacquie,
and for Christina when she is a little older,
with love

One

With a scrunch of tires on gravel, Mr. Brookes slowed the station wagon to a stop in front of the rambling white frame ranch house, tooted the horn to let them know we had arrived and eased his lanky frame from behind the wheel. "Here we are, Tim, the Circle Diamond Ranch, your summer home away from home."

I was numb with culture shock. Whatever happened to pavement and traffic noises and jostling crowds? How could anybody be expected to live with nothing in any direction but space and silence and sunshine?

I stared at the scene around me. To my left, rolling, tree-covered hills climbed gently toward a ridge of low mountains. To my right, identical multi-greened hills dropped away to the green-black waters of the Thompson River. In between were fields like patches on a quilt, each fenced to separate it from its neighbors. Some of the fields were dark green with some kind of crop. Others must have been cut recently because they still wore an irregular pattern of hay bales. The rest were dotted with brown spots that even I recognized as grazing cows. The only action in the whole landscape was three slowly moving figures on horseback making their way down the fence line.

I raised my eyes skyward. "Beam me up, Scotty," I pleaded silently. "There's no intelligent life down here." How could there be in all this fresh air and ear-shattering silence? How was I ever going to survive a whole summer of . . .

"Tim, this is Doug." Mr. Brookes's words jolted me back to reality.

I opened the door of the station wagon and clambered out. "Hi," I said, gazing up at a tall, dark-haired figure.

Again I was in shock. Not culture shock this time, but social, and not just because Doug Brookes looked like a model for bodybuilding ads with a tan that would do a Hollywood lifeguard proud. It was his composure that threw me. What I wouldn't give for that calm, self-confident look.

I bet there was no way Doug Brookes would ever have got himself grounded for two weeks because he was too embarrassed to admit to the guys that his folks had imposed a midnight curfew. And if he was ever called down to the principal's office — which he probably wasn't — I bet he didn't come all over guilt and embarrassment.

Mind you, a little voice inside my head pointed out, by the time I was Doug's age maybe I'd have managed to acquire some self-confidence, too. But I knew the little voice was kidding. Two years wouldn't make that much difference.

I continued to stare. From what my folks had said, I knew Doug was eighteen, but he could have passed for older. He even shaved regularly. You could tell from the smooth, weathered look of his cheeks.

Pretending my own face tickled, I put up a hand and rubbed my mouth, so nobody would notice the blush of pale hairs on my upper lip — all I'd managed to produce so far.

Doug was surveying the mountain of gear I'd jammed into the back of the wagon. His eyebrows lifted fractionally. "Are you sure you didn't forget anything?"

"Probably. But I make it a rule to travel light."

The hint of a smile tugged at the corners of his mouth, but he didn't say anything.

We pulled everything out and dumped it into the center of the drive. Doug picked up my sleeping bag and suitcase and started for the house. I followed with my guitar in one hand, a fly rod in the other and my brand-new matched set of golf clubs hooked around my neck. In spite of what my dad said, there was no way I was going to leave the clubs in Winnipeg after I had finally managed to break ninety with them the day before I left. That left my tackle box, but I decided it would have to stay where it was for the moment, in the middle of the driveway.

Mrs. Brookes was waiting at the door. Before I had a chance to duck she grabbed me and planted a kiss on my ear. I think she meant it for my cheek, but at the last minute I managed to dodge a little. Did getting kissed by someone I didn't even know ever make me feel silly, particularly when, out of the corner of my eye, I could see Doug grinning at me. I didn't know where to look and my ear felt all hot.

"We're glad to have you, Tim," Mrs. Brookes said. "Take your things upstairs. Hilary is up there. She'll show you your room."

Doug had already taken my other stuff up, so I followed. Then for the third time in ten minutes I was in shock. Emotional this time.

Whoever said that the most beautiful girls in the world lived in Winnipeg hadn't seen Hilary Brookes. She was so willowy I bet if I put my hands around her waist my fingers would have touched. She had wavy brown hair that came half-way down her back and the same great tan that Doug had. Best of all, she was my age. My folks had told me that, too.

"Here's your room." Her voice was soft and low-pitched like one of those seductive girl spies on the afternoon TV movies. "Dinner will be ready soon, so come down as soon as you've unpacked."

I watched her go. Then I bumped my way over to the bed and dropped everything in a heap on the floor. I'd go back for the tackle box in a minute, I promised myself. I had an idea Mr. Brookes might not be too pleased if he drove over it and punctured a tire, but I needed a second to recover.

I kicked off my shoes and stretched full length on the bed. Then I looked at my watch. Six o'clock. That would be eight in Winnipeg. Brad and Rory would have spent the afternoon making a neat little profit playing a buck a game at the video arcade, and now they'd be on their way to one of the drive-ins in Brad's truck. Unless, of course, Rory's mom had lifted the ban and was letting them use her car, but that wasn't too likely. Not after the drag race we had down North Main Street a week ago.

Even thinking about it made me grin. If there's one thing old Brad is really good at, it's organizing things like drag races so nobody gets caught. It's a talent he's got, or maybe it comes with age, because he's a year older than the rest of us. In any case, he seems to know where every prowl car is at every given moment.

Just around ten o'clock is the time Brad likes best, when there's enough traffic on the streets to make a race challenging, but not enough to make it impossible. The area he likes best is along North Main Street. That's because the coffee-shop owners there offer the cops free coffee in the evenings to encourage them to stop by. Brad takes a couple of runs past the half dozen spots the cops like best to make sure the boys in blue have gone in for their evening break, and the race is on.

But last Friday night he blew it. The three regular North Main prowl cars were parked just where they were supposed to be, outside three of the coffee shops, but Brad hadn't counted on an unmarked cruiser driven by an out-of-uniform police woman.

I was riding in Rory's car. While the cop was busy pulling Brad over, we managed to take off and get lost, but it was a wonder we hadn't given the show away because we had nearly died laughing at the expression on poor Brad's face.

I continued staring at the white ceiling.

On second thought, Brad and Rory and the rest

of the guys probably weren't at the drive-in after all, because chances were Brad wouldn't be driving again, either. But they'd be somewhere, the park if nowhere else, and wherever they were they'd be having a lot of laughs.

What I wouldn't have given to be with them.

I let my breath out in a long, dreary groan. So much for the ten weeks of glorious holidays I had been looking forward to since last September. Instead, what do I get stuck with? Ten weeks in exile, with no time off for good behavior.

Out of the corner of my eye I could see the mound of my gear waiting to be unpacked.

Sixteen's a heck of an age, I decided, returning my attention to the ceiling. A couple of years younger and you don't mind so much being pushed around by your folks. A couple of years older and they don't do it any more. But at sixteen you're a puppet dancing to their music.

The stupid thing about this tune was that it was unnecessary. I'd tried to tell my dad that, but explaining to parents is a little like trying to talk under water. Not too much gets through.

Dad said I was being sent west for the summer because I was too easily led, afraid to stand up for myself and for what I thought was right. I couldn't make him see that being easily led had nothing to do with it. I just hate arguments. Years ago I discovered how much easier it is to let other people have their way if they want it all that badly. That way there's no hassle and no unpleasantness. There's also no nagging guilty feeling if we end up doing something a bit borderline, like ganging up on old Tubs or passing around a few answers on a test. There's no way a person can feel guilty when he knows he didn't think up the idea. Besides, if he doesn't go along with what everybody else wants to do it looks as if he's criticizing or something.

But my folks can't understand that.

I had known for a while that they had some doubts about me. More than once they had come right out and admitted that my two little sisters were a lot less of a headache. And every time Mom cleaned my room lately, she had a good look around. My magazines ended up in a different order and my desk drawer looked different. But I didn't pay too much attention. Even though my folks and I don't see exactly eye to eye on music and manners and clothes and things like that, we still have a pretty good relationship.

At least we did till Rory's party. That shattered it.

The party was on the day after school ended. It was a great party. When it finally broke up about one in the morning, all I could think of was how great it was going to feel to hit the sack for twelve straight hours. I managed to ease the front door open without it squeaking and waking everybody up, and congratulated myself on being so smart. Then I tiptoed in and started to close it.

"I refuse to sit back and allow you to drift into trouble with that gang you chum around with," my dad boomed out in his parade-square voice.

"P-pardon?" He startled me so badly I dropped my key.

"We've just been awakened by a telephone call from the Gleasons," he went on, and I knew right then I was in for trouble. The Gleasons have a reputation for exaggerating everything and getting hysterical. "Jimmy has just been brought home by the police after a wild party at Rory's house, and he says you were there, too."

Good old Jimmy. I could have strangled him. "It wasn't wild, Dad," I began.

"Then what do you call it when the police are summoned because of the noise and have to fight their way into the house through a mountain of empty beer bottles and a haze of marijuana smoke?"

"There wasn't any marijuana," I insisted. "And all those empties had been left from a party Rory's folks had a couple of nights ago. We were drinking Cokes . . . mostly . . ." I added the last word under my breath so he wouldn't hear me but so I wouldn't be telling a lie.

"That's not what the Gleasons told me."

I could tell from the look on his face that it was useless to argue, but it made me mad because what I was saying was ninety-nine percent true. All but two cases of those empties had been left from Rory's folks' party, and there hadn't been any marijuana. Not a single joint. A couple of weeks ago, maybe, but not this time.

"School has been over for exactly one day and already you're in trouble," he had gone on, using the same long-suffering tone he uses on Spook when she growls at the postman. "There's a lot of temptation for a boy your age in a city like Winnipeg. If you haven't the gumption to steer clear of it, then you'd better spend the summer someplace where you won't be tempted."

That someplace was the Circle Diamond ranch, between Cache Creek and Ashcroft at the entrance to British Columbia's Cariboo.

I stopped staring at the ceiling and looked around the room that was to be my home away from home, as Mr. Brookes had put it, until Labor Day. More utilitarian than luxurious, I decided, eyeing the varnished chest of drawers with the square mirror hanging overtop, the chintz-covered armchair by the window with a metal goosenecked reading lamp sitting in school-teacher fashion behind the left corner, and the solid iron bedstead. I bounced up and down on the mattress. Not bad. Not too soft and not too hard. Then I smiled, because that reminded me of Goldilocks in the bears' house, and Goldilocks reminded me of Hilary. Reverse negative on the hair color, of course, but the rest was the same.

I snuggled deeper into the mattress. At least there was one ray of light in this incarceration. If worse came to worst, I could spend the whole ten weeks in bed, dreaming about what it would be like to have a girlfriend who looked like Hilary Brookes.

I stopped snuggling, for a daydream was all it was likely to be. During the course of my sixteen years I'd discovered that gorgeous girls don't exactly line up for the chance to smile at guys who are skinny and awkward, who can never think of clever things to say and who blush as soon as a girl notices them. At least they don't in Winnipeg, so chances were pretty good they wouldn't in British Columbia, either.

"Dinner, Tim!" Mrs. Brookes's voice floated up to me.

I jumped off the bed. I took a fast check in the mirror. For the first time I wondered if I should have listened to my dad when he told me not to get such a short haircut. Not only was mine about as short as possible but it was spiked to boot. Compared with the haircuts everybody else on the ranch seemed to favor, mine looked a bit like . . .

"Coming, Tim?"

There was nothing I could do about it now. I would just have to hope Hilary was a Billy Idol fan.

As I stepped over the mountain of stuff that still sat patiently in the middle of the rug, it occurred to me that maybe I should have unpacked. If Mrs. Brookes came up and saw the mess she might be a bit angry. But the next moment I told myself not to be dumb. After all, what was the hurry? I had ten whole weeks to finish my unpacking.

Two

"Do you ride, Tim?" Hilary asked me as soon as we were seated at the big table. The ranch hands and the Brookes family all eat together in the dining room, but that night there was only a handful of men at the table because it was payday. Mr. Brookes always gives the hands a few days off after payday, and most of them had left right after work to get a head start on their holiday.

"No," I admitted, helping myself to a huge piece of roast beef from the platter in front of me before passing it on.

"Have you ever tried?"

I shook my head. I accepted the bowl of mashed potatoes from Hilary and added a large fluffy white mound to the beef on my plate.

"Do you think you could teach him, Doug?" Hilary asked, looking across the table at her brother. Her glance returned to me. "There's a big rodeo at Falkland on the long weekend at the beginning of August. Everybody's entering something. If Doug teaches you to rope, you could —"

"There's not much chance of Tim or anybody else learning to rope in five weeks," Doug interrupted, smiling indulgently at his sister. "Roping takes years." Then his dark eyes started to tease. "However, how about both of you entering the jousting?"

Hilary gave him the long-suffering look that sisters reserve exclusively for older brothers. "If you're so brave, I'm surprised you haven't signed up."

"Actually, I would have," Doug replied, struggling to keep his expression serious, "but I couldn't shake the feeling that it would be an awful shame for my little sister to grow up an only child."

Hilary laughed. "Will you at least teach Tim to ride by then?" Her face was serious once again. "Otherwise he won't be able to take part in anything."

At that moment the roast beef and mashed potatoes that were circulating reached Doug's side of the table. With more attention on his plate than his sister, he replied absently, "I guess if Tim wants to give it a try, I could teach him to ride before the rodeo."

Right then I should have had the sense to say no thanks. But Doug went on to explain that it would have to wait a bit till the hands were back from their payday holiday and all the hay had been brought in, so I let it go. What was the point in sweating the small stuff? There was no way Doug was going to give top priority to teaching some city kid to ride; I was willing to bet he would never think of it again. If I was wrong, that would be the time to tell him thanks but no thanks. So I let it go and asked instead, "What's this jousting thing?"

"The newest method of instant suicide," Doug replied between bites.

"Silly," Hilary said. Then to me, "Don't let my nose-to-the-grindstone brother put you off. Jousting is terrific. It's a modern version of the contests the knights used to hold in the Middle Ages, with lances and swords and everything. The Falkland rodeo is going to include an official international jousting tournament."

Games on horseback with swords and lances sounded sort of dumb to me, but I didn't think I should say so.

Doug washed down a huge mouthful of roast beef with a half glass of milk. He was watching his sister. His eyebrows raised a little. "By any chance could that remark you made the other day about wanting to be a nurse have anything to do with this sudden desire to get me to joust? You wouldn't be trying to line up your own personal corpse to practice on, would you?"

Hilary burst out laughing.

I felt a twinge of envy. I wouldn't have minded having Hilary look at me the way she was looking at her brother.

"Wait till you see my little sister do her stuff at the rodeo," Doug continued, turning to me. His voice was teasing, but I could see the pride in his eyes. "When she goes around those barrels she sets up such a wind that all the spectators lose their hats."

Hilary made a face at him.

I couldn't help but think of my own little sisters. If they were closer to me in age, would we have this kind of relationship, or was it different when you lived in the country? I didn't know, but I decided Doug was pretty lucky.

As soon as supper was over Doug said he had some work to do. Hilary went to the kitchen to help her mom make some pies for the next day's lunch, since the two regular cooks had gone with their husbands on the payday holiday. There didn't seem much for me to do, so I picked up the *Ashcroft Journal* and looked at the sports page.

I couldn't believe it. Not one single word about the Argo defensive end who was supposed to be traded to the Bombers. Weren't people out here interested in important things?

I put the paper down and stared out at the darkness. Whatever Brad and Rory were doing, I sure wished I was doing it with them.

I took my time going down for breakfast the next morning because the house was so quiet I figured everybody must be sleeping, but it turned out they had gone somewhere. My place was set at the big oak table with half a pitcher of orange juice and three different boxes of cereal for me to choose from, so I sat down and helped myself. Before I was down to the milk at the bottom of the cereal bowl Hilary came in from the kitchen carrying a platter.

"I hope you're hungry, Tim. I've cooked you some bacon and eggs." The bacon was still sizzling on the hot platter as she put it in front of me, and the eggs were a deep yellow with the edges slightly browned, just the way I like them. "If you're looking for your tackle box, Doug told me to tell you he put it on the porch. I guess he was afraid it might get run over in the driveway."

She tried to keep a straight face, but I caught the gleam of laughter in her eyes and I smiled back. I was embarrassed. I'd forgotten all about that tackle box.

"Thanks. Where is everybody?"

"Mom's gone to town. Everybody else is haying the south meadow."

I took a big mouthful of the bacon and eggs. I vaguely remembered some talk at dinner last night about haying, but I hadn't paid much attention because I knew it had nothing to do with me. There was no way I was getting up at five-thirty in the morning to go haying. I had come to the ranch for a holiday, not for a job. Maybe later on I might join in some of the ranch activities if I had nothing else to do, but for the moment my top priority was catching up on my sleep. Besides, Mr. and Mrs. Brookes wouldn't expect me to behave like a ranch hand. They were personal friends of my folks, and the arrangement had been that I would visit them this summer, then maybe Hilary would come to Winnipeg next year and visit us. Doug, too, of course, if he wanted to, but I didn't figure he would. From what I'd seen of him, I figured he would say he was needed on the ranch.

"Nobody wanted to make you get up too early on your first morning," Hilary went on, "but I promised as soon as you were through breakfast we'd go lend them a hand."

I swallowed another big mouthful. "Thanks," I said as soon as my mouth was empty, "but I'm not that interested in haying. Is there any good fishing in the creek?"

A funny expression came over her face, but the next moment she was smiling again. "There's terrific fishing, Tim. Just follow the creek down to where it narrows. You'll see some big rocks there. Doug says he has the best luck when he stands on the rocks and casts."

"Want to come with me?"

"I can't. I'm going to help with the haying for a while, then I've got to come back and get lunch ready. The cooks are gone for two days at least, and Mom won't be back from town till four."

I finished every bite of the bacon and eggs, and two crispy pieces of toast as well, then I got up from the table. "Thanks for the breakfast. That was good. I guess I'll try my luck on those rocks."

As I turned to go I thought I caught a glimpse of that same puzzled expression, but I must have imagined it because Hilary just picked up my dishes and told me to have a good day.

I did — sort of.

I didn't stand on the rocks as she suggested because it was too hot. I sat on them instead, and dangled my feet in the water while I waited for some adventuresome kokanee to come along and snap at my lure. I tried to imagine what Brad and Rory would be doing. Playing football with a whole bunch of guys in the school yard if it wasn't too hot, I decided, and if it was, listening to tapes in Rory's basement.

Both Rory's folks work, so he can have the guys in and make as much noise as he wants. They'd probably be sprawled on the couch and floor, with their feet on the coffee table. Rory would have set out a bowl of potato chips and some Cokes and thrown a heavy metal record on the stereo.

At that moment I would have settled for the summer job Dad had lined up for me as a gas jockey at the full-service Esso station on Ellice Avenue. Dad knows the guy who runs the place. Even before Rory's party he had said it would be good for me to have something to do for the summer, but I had told him no thanks. There was no way I wanted to tie myself up pumping gas and washing windshields while all the rest of the kids were having a ball.

For once my dad had been pretty reasonable. He said okay — that I had only just turned sixteen so maybe I should have one more free summer before starting the lifelong work grind.

But that job sure would have been better than where I had ended up. At least if I had been working I'd have had my evenings and weekends free, and that was the only time that mattered anyway, because most of the guys stayed in bed till noon.

They were lucky. My mom always boots me out by ten-thirty or eleven. It makes me mad. What's there to do that early in the day? But she refuses to listen. For some reason she seems to have a thing about getting up in the morning. That was one reason that out here I wasn't gonna . . .

Something tugged at my line and I forgot all about everything but the pretty little trout I had snagged, about half a kilogram, probably. I played him carefully for a bit, then reeled him in.

For a second after I took the hook out of his mouth I held him in my fingers and looked at him. That's the part I don't like about fishing — the business of bonking the fish on the head. But there's not much point in fishing at all if you just throw everything back, so I gritted my teeth and konked him with the little wooden bat I keep in my tackle box. At least it was quick and he didn't feel anything. Then I laid him in the shade on the shore and went back to fishing. Only this time I stood up. I decided if I went about it in a more energetic fashion I might catch enough for everyone's breakfast the next morning, and that might take away the puzzled look on Hilary's face, which was still disturbing me.

I was right. On both counts. Not only did I catch four more fish after I decided to stand up, but Hilary was really pleased when I handed them to her. "Thought these might do for breakfast tomorrow," I said.

She smiled at me without any trace of that funny look. "One apiece. That's terrific. I'll tell Mom to save the biggest one for you when you come down."

"Maybe I should come down early with everyone else tomorrow." The words were out before I could stop them. "That way it won't be so much work for your mom."

Now she really smiled.

Three

I kept my word and struggled down for breakfast at a quarter to six. It wasn't easy. Then one look around the breakfast table convinced me it wasn't worth it, either. Everyone looked exactly the way I felt, which was terrible.

They had been haying steadily for about two weeks, for the last week working almost around the clock. All the fields had been cut and raked, but now the hay had to be baled and stored before the rain that was hovering on the horizon decided to pay a visit. If the hay got wet it would rot in the barn before the winter was over.

I found out a little later that they went through this crisis three times a summer, once with each hay crop. This was just the first for that year.

"Good morning, Tim," Mr. Brookes greeted me. "Do you smell those fish of yours frying? It's a good thing you came down early or there wouldn't have been any left for you."

I smiled at him and looked around the dining room. Aside from Doug and Mr. Brookes and me, there were just two other guys. "Aren't the men back yet?" I asked.

"Not till the day after tomorrow," Mr. Brookes replied.

"But I thought you still had a lot of hay to get in."

"We do."

"Then why give the men time off right in the middle?"

He smiled patiently. "After you've been here awhile you'll find out that ranching is a series of emergencies. There's always something that has to be done before the weather changes. If we canceled holidays for that reason no one would ever get a day off."

"What about you and Doug?"

His smile broadened. "That's different. We're management. That gives us the right to work all the time."

Doug laughed. "I'll second that."

I glanced across the table to where Hilary was sitting beside her father. She was smiling at me. All of a sudden I couldn't believe my ears. A voice that sounded suspiciously like mine was saying, "Then maybe you could use an extra hand."

"We certainly could," Mr. Brookes replied.

I stole another look at Hilary. From the expression on her face you would have thought I was something special.

I turned my attention to breakfast. Did that fish ever taste good. Must be some particular brand of trout they grow in British Columbia.

As soon as breakfast was over I went haying. By seven o'clock I knew how Doug had come by his Charles Atlas physique. By eight I'd decided that if haying was the only way to acquire it, then it wasn't all that necessary to my happiness.

I tried to make up my mind exactly what I hated most about haying — the heat, the boredom, or the way the dust seemed to rise out of the stubble and choke off my breathing. Maybe it was the blazing sun making my skin so dry I was afraid to smile; or the way the stubble pricked through my socks into my ankles, which was probably why all the other guys were wearing boots. Or maybe it was just that the whole thing was such unbelievably hard work.

Eighteen-kilogram bales don't sound like much, but when you've restricted your physical activity to the odd baseball game and pedaling your bike to school on nice flat Winnipeg streets, heaving bales of hay onto a wagon is no joke. By the end of the first hour I felt like Old Father Time at New Year's. When I tried to straighten up I had to go by stages.

By ten o'clock we'd worked our way down to a sort of dogleg at the end of the main field. The wagon with the tractor pulling it was at the opening into the bigger field. Hilary was driving the tractor, Doug and Mr. Brookes were collecting the last few bales in the main field, while the two hands and I were starting to work the dogleg.

The big field had been bad enough, but at least a slight breeze had kept the mosquitoes down. The dogleg was closed in by bushes and trees, and the mosquitoes were in undisputed possession. I decided not to fight them for it. Everyone was too busy tossing bales around like baseballs at a Blue Jays' training camp to pay much attention to me, so I drifted into the trees and headed back to the ranch.

Was it ever great to get inside where it was cool

and free of mosquitoes. I stretched out on my bed with my pile of *Sports Illustrated*s from home. I had read them all before, but that didn't matter.

One story told about this kid who made a fortune with his own peanut concession at a baseball park in the States somewhere. I started to laugh because Rory and Brad and I did the same sort of thing last month. We offered to raise some money for the school track team by selling homemade Popsicles at the District Secondary School track meet. Brad was the one who came up with the idea, and it was great. If the school hadn't gone all narrow-minded on us, not only could we have made some cash for our team, but there was a real possibility we'd have played a major role in engineering Centerville Senior Secondary's first ever district sports championship.

We called our Popsicles Olympic Gold and sold them for a quarter to the athletes from all the other schools. Not to our own athletes, though — we refused to sell any to them, but people from other schools could buy as many as they wanted.

They bought lots. Partly because it was such a great day, hotter than thirty degrees Celsius. But the taste had even more to do with it.

If our school had just minded its business and allowed us to run ours, everything would have been great, but when a couple of the best athletes who had eaten three or four started having a little trouble staying in their lanes, the vice-principal got suspicious.

We tried to tell him that nobody but visiting athletes could buy Popsicles, but he refused to listen. He didn't even cough up a quarter, he just helped himself. Two seconds later our Popsicle concession was history. One bite was all he needed to determine that Olympic Gold Popsicles were one hundred percent Molson Canadian.

You'd think schools would encourage original thinking, but not the one we go to.

I finished the *Sports Illustrated*s.

I tried to sleep.

It seemed like hours before there was a sound anywhere in the ranch house. I found out afterward that Mrs. Brookes had packed a lunch and taken it out to the gang in the hayfield so they wouldn't have to come all the way in, but at the time I just figured nobody was hungry except me. There didn't seem much point in bothering to go down and rustle something for myself in the heat, so I stayed where I was. Before long I fell asleep.

"We appreciated your help this morning, Tim," Mr. Brookes told me at dinner. "I know it's pretty hard work until you're used to it, but every day it'll get easier. There's a lot of hay to bring in yet."

"We'll need at least three, maybe four more days," Doug put in. "The question is whether or not the weather will hold that long."

I vaguely remember hearing the early gong the next morning. There's a triangle hanging just outside the kitchen door that Mrs. Brookes rings at five-thirty. You could probably hear it all the way to Winnipeg on a clear morning. It means *get up*. Then she rings it again at five forty-five, and that time it means *if you don't come, you'll have to go to work without any breakfast*. I heard that gong, too, but I didn't pay any attention. I'd been sent to the ranch for the summer and I'd stick it out, but that didn't mean I had to feel responsible for its successful operation. Probably the others liked haying, otherwise they wouldn't be ranchers. But I didn't. I preferred to sleep. So I did, until noon, every day for the next three days.

But by the fourth morning I was beginning to get restless. It was Saturday. I had been at the ranch six full days by then — for the last four ignored by everybody. From six in the morning till six at night I was left by myself with nothing to do but reread the same old sports magazines.

The evenings were no better. After supper everyone just sat around and beefed about their aching muscles. Even Hilary joined the complaint department. How anyone that delicate-looking could lift eighteen-kilogram bales I wasn't sure, but apparently she alternated driving the tractor with heaving bales whenever the men were short-handed or the weather threatened to break.

But the previous evening someone had said the present horrendous session of haying was finally over. It would be six weeks at least before the torture would have to be undertaken again. Now maybe people could be normal and sociable again. Somebody might even go fishing with me, or play eighteen holes of golf.

With that hope to bolster me I went downstairs in search of food and companionship.

Though it was almost eleven o'clock, my place was still set at the table. I helped myself to orange juice and two bowls of cereal. Bacon and eggs would have been nice. I could hear someone in the kitchen and for a minute I debated going out and asking whoever it was to cook me some.

I decided against it.

I didn't want the guys to come in for lunch in

another hour or so and find my breakfast dishes still on the table, so I picked up my bowl and glass in one hand, the orange-juice pitcher in the other, caught the cereal box under my arm and headed for the kitchen.

I'd been right about somebody being there. It was Hilary. "Hey! Terrific!" I beamed at her. "Now that the haying is over people can take it easy again. Did you sleep in, too?" I was about to set my dishes in the sink, but at the blaze of anger on Hilary's face I practically dropped them. What had I said, for Pete's sake?

Then I realized she was so tired from all that haying she would have flared up if it had been December twenty-fifth and I had wished her Merry Christmas. Which was proof right there that she shouldn't be doing it.

"What's Doug up to this sunny Saturday morning?" I asked brightly, changing the subject in the hope that her bad mood would pass. I figured if I kept smiling at her she'd have to smile back.

I was wrong. Not only didn't she smile, she also didn't answer.

I tried again. "D'you think he'd like to go fishing?" I knew I should wait for him to ask me, since he was the host and two years older and everything, only from the looks of things he wasn't going to, and fishing isn't much fun alone.

If it's possible for ice to turn colder, that's what Hilary's expression did. She looked as if I had just suggested that Doug take off for a month's vacation in Hawaii.

"I'm sure Doug would love to go fishing," she said with stiff formality. "However, he has a ranch to help run."

"But somebody said last night that the hay crop was all in."

"In case you haven't noticed, bringing in the hay crop is only one small part of a ranching operation. Right now Doug is mending fence."

I didn't understand, and I told her so.

"Different cattle are kept in different sections," she explained, her voice still icy. "Doug and some of the hands are mending the dividing fences that have become weakened over the winter."

"Oh." That sounded like less work than haying, and I had to do something to get that look off her face. "Do you think they'd like some help?" I felt heroic and self-sacrificing as the words came out.

But it wasn't like five days earlier when I volunteered for that suicide mission in the hayfield; this time Hilary didn't even smile. "You can ask them at lunch time." She turned on her heel and disappeared.

I was confused. What had I done that was so bad?

I waited until the guys came in for lunch, then went into the dining room with them as if I hadn't just finished breakfast.

"Hello, Tim," Mr. Brookes said as he moved by me. Doug nodded vaguely. Nobody else paid any attention, which wasn't surprising. Since the men had come back from their payday holiday I had only seen them at dinnertime.

I found an empty seat at the end of the table next to Doug and sat down. Fortunately everybody was too hungry to talk much, because it took me a minute or two to get my courage up. "Like a hand with the fences?" I managed at last.

Doug looked up from his spaghetti. He studied me in silence, a reserved, almost withdrawn expression on his face. "No, thanks," he said at last, and returned his attention to his lunch.

Does an answer like that ever leave a person high and dry. I didn't know where to look, and I went all hot and funny inside.

Fortunately Mr. Brookes had heard the exchange. "Of course they can use you, Tim," he said. "Good of you to offer. Take him along after lunch, Doug, and show him what to do."

The line of Doug's jaw seemed to tighten. "We're not mending any more fence this afternoon," he replied evenly. "It's too hot. We're going to finish moving those irrigation pipes, then knock off for a couple of hours till it's cooler."

"Tim can help with the pipes." Mr. Brooke's tone made it clear it was an order.

Doug's face tightened even more. He opened his mouth to say something.

Obviously his dad was determined to avoid any unpleasantness. Before Doug could speak, Mr. Brookes continued brightly, "The pipes won't take long. After you've finished why don't you use the rest of the afternoon to get Tim started learning to ride? Hilary's right, he should learn before the rodeo, and that's just four weeks away."

From the way Doug had been looking at me ever since I came into the dining room I knew that the last thing he wanted was to teach me to do anything, and I waited for him to make an excuse.

But all of a sudden the hard, set look along his jawline softened, and a thoughtful look came into his eyes. He nodded slowly. "I guess I could do that. I'll get Gus and Billy to lend me a hand."

That first time the subject had been raised I had let it pass. This time, however, was different. This was the time to say no thanks clearly and firmly. If I refused lessons I couldn't get roped into any rodeo. Maybe I wouldn't have all that much fun, but at least I'd stay in one piece.

I had to be tactful but I also had to be honest. I had to speak up and make it clear that riding wasn't something I wanted to learn.

I took a deep breath.

"Okay," I said.

Four

Right after lunch I went out with Doug to the north section. That's where I met Gus and Billy.

Gus David and Billy Jack are ranch hands. They're about Doug's age, I guess, but they act younger. They're lanky, blue-jeaned and always dusty.

Gus is Doug's favorite. He's not a bad-looking kid. Too thin, but he probably looks thinner than he is because of his long, straight hair.

The first thing I noticed about Gus and Billy was the way they could enjoy silence together. Most people feel they have to be talking all the time, but Gus and Billy can go for hours sometimes not saying anything, just sharing a nod or a look or an occasional smile.

The second thing I noticed was their names. I'd never met anyone with two first names before, but it seems to be fairly common with the native Canadians in the west. It's nice. I like it — Gus David, Billy Jack, Charlie Paul. It gives a feeling of family belonging.

"We've got a new hand," Doug announced as we met up with Gus and Billy. "First he's going to learn all about laying irrigation pipes, then he wants to learn to ride."

Gus and Billy looked first at Doug, then at me, then at Doug again. They didn't speak.

"Do you think that palomino in the barn would be a good way to start him off?" Doug's voice was casual.

I saw the corners of Billy's eyes crinkle slightly as if he was smiling inside, but there was no other sign of expression.

Gus's face remained impassive. "Guess so," he answered at last.

"Then let's take care of these pipes," Doug said, heading off at a brisk pace. Gus and Billy matched strides with him while I sauntered along behind.

One of them must have said something funny because they all laughed. I envied them. I wished Brad and Rory were there.

"Grab the end of that pipe," Doug told me as we reached the north pasture. "Stand still and we'll pivot around you."

I stopped thinking about Brad and Rory and did as he said.

Doug and Gus picked up the far end of the aluminum pipe and I practically dropped my end on my foot. Aluminum is supposed to be light, but those pipes weren't. Probably because they were a good twenty centimeters in diameter, and every one of them had some water left inside it somewhere.

There were about two dozen lengths of pipe to move, and by the time we were finished I was dead. I sat down right where I was. Gus and Billy moved over to a little patch of shade beside a baler parked at the end of the field and lit cigarettes. Doug joined them but he didn't smoke.

When Gus and Billy had butted their cigarettes on the ground, Doug got to his feet. "Come on," he said, looking at me. He headed toward the ranch house and once again Gus and Billy matched strides with him.

As soon as we reached the barn I should have realized something was up. Gus and Billy made a beeline for the corral fence and took their places on the top bar, grinning from ear to ear. It was the first time I'd seen them smile and that in itself should have been a warning, but I was too dumb to catch on.

I followed Doug into the barn. In a standing stall at the far end was a palomino quarter horse.

One of the first questions I'd asked after I arrived at the Circle Diamond was why so many of the ranch horses were called "quarter horses." If I'd known the Brookeses well enough to make jokes I'd have asked what the other three quarters was. But since I didn't, I kept the question serious. Hilary was the one who explained. They were called quarter horses, she said, because they held the record against all other breeds for quarter-mile races. I guess considering how often a cattleman needs a horse that's fast on short spurts — to head off a cow that's trying to leave the herd, or to get to an open corral gate ahead of some unbroken pony — it's no wonder quarter horses are so popular.

I watched while Doug threw a saddle on the palomino and put a bridle over his head. I moved closer and in my best television-western style ran a hand down the side of his neck. "Nice-looking animal. What's his name?"

Maybe Doug didn't hear. Anyway he didn't answer. "Lead him outside and I'll give you a leg up," he directed.

A little hesitantly I moved toward the barn doorway. I got as far as one rein-length. Then I stopped. The other end of the rein, the opposite end to the one in my hand, wasn't moving. It was attached to an immovable object whose four legs seemed permanently planted where they stood.

"Come on, fella," I pleaded in an undertone. I could imagine the jeers that would come from the three outside if I couldn't even lead my horse out of the barn.

Maybe quarter horses don't like to be laughed at any more than I do, or maybe this one just felt sorry for me. In any case he unplanted his feet and walked quietly along after me.

"Put your foot in my hands," Doug directed as I stood facing the side of the horse, both hands holding onto the leather of the saddle.

The next second I was struggling to keep from sailing over the top and onto the ground on the other side. I grabbed for the saddle horn. Maybe that's what it's there for. That's what I used it for, anyway.

I was still trying to catch my breath when Doug began a rapid rundown of the finer points of riding. All I caught was "show him who's boss." Then Doug let go of the reins.

The horse stood motionless.

So did I.

"At a standstill, you're a star," Doug drawled evenly. "Now let's try a little movement. He's lazy, so give him a good jab in the flanks."

I stretched my legs out sideways and brought both heels in hard against the horse's ribs.

What happened after that is a little hazy. I remember thinking that I'd been wrong about the horn. It hadn't been put there to help a person stay in the saddle. It had been put there as an instrument for self-destruction. Just two or three more good hits against it and I'd be mashed to a pulp. But fortunately before that happened I was on the ground, face down in the dirt, unable to move or speak because the breath had been knocked out of me, but alive, at least. All I could hear above the ringing in my ears were shouts of laughter.

It was Doug who picked me up under the arms and dropped me on my rump to get the air back in my lungs.

"Thanks," I managed to gasp.

"A few minutes ago you asked me that palomino's name," Doug said. "It's Trouble. As long as you urge him along gently, he's a lamb. But there isn't a man on the ranch who could boot him in the ribs the way you just did and stay on his back."

"Thanks a whole lot."

Doug was still grinning. "Come on. If there aren't any bones broken we'll get you a horse you really can learn to ride on."

I felt myself gingerly. Nothing semed to be broken. I could even walk in a dazed sort of way.

The new horse Doug and Gus saddled for me

was a mare named Brownie, and this time as Doug helped me up he gave me a little more information about what I should do, like gripping with my knees, neck reining and only holding the horn in emergencies. The whole exercise was an emergency, in my opinion, so I nodded agreement, then commissioned one hand to do nothing but clutch the horn. Doug, Gus and Billy all tried to convince me to let go, but I didn't trust them.

That was lesson number one.

Every day after that for ten horrendous days, after working with Doug and Gus and Billy in the mornings mending fences and moving irrigation pipes, I spent the afternoons practicing riding. By the tenth day I had managed to master the basics: remaining in the saddle and coaxing my horse into going where I wanted her to — so long as she didn't have any alternative, that is. I still hadn't mastered what to do in the event of a conflict of interest.

Then Doug suggested maybe I should have a go at roping.

If the ornery steers had played fair I might have learned the trick of that, too, but Circle Diamond cattle can't have heard of the Marquis of Queensbury. When they're running and you throw a rope ahead of them, they stop short. When they're standing still and you throw right at them, they take off at a gallop. Doug had been right when he'd told Hilary it would take more than a few weeks to teach me to rope. It would take more than a few years.

But at least I'd learned vaguely how to ride — thanks to a couple of rolls of adhesive bandage.

That, I discovered, was the secret of the exercise. If a person wraps enough bandage around the inside of his knees, and pads as many of the other contact spots as he can reach, the whole thing becomes, as the dentists say, practically painless.

Five

I figured that if I struggled out of bed in the middle of the night for a week and a half, made myself useful digging postholes and heaving irrigation pipes and risked my neck daily trying to learn to ride, Hilary might let me out of the deep-freeze.

For a day or two right at the start it looked as if she was going to. On that first Saturday when Doug reported in living technicolor every detail of my attempt to ride Trouble, she actually smiled and started chattering as if we could be friends after all. But something must have reversed the process because once again the ice age set in.

I think it started up again on Monday night when I told her about Gus and Billy.

That morning Doug, Gus, Billy and I had been building a new piece of fence. It must have been more than thirty-two degrees Celsius, and we'd been digging postholes and sawing timber for a couple of hours without a break.

"Let's take five, guys," Doug had suggested.

He didn't have to say it twice. All four of us flopped down in the shade beside a bunch of scrubby willow bushes.

I was gazing at the sky, chewing a piece of grass and making pictures out of the clouds, when Karl drove up.

Karl was the ranch foreman. He must have had another name at some point but I never heard it. Surnames suggest family and belonging, and somehow that sort of thing didn't seem to fit with Karl.

"What d'you think this is, third week at the health spa?" Karl bellowed from the open half-ton truck he was driving along the fence line. Even in the short time I had been at the Circle Diamond I had discovered that Karl bellowed a lot. "Let's try a little work for a change."

"If you'd bothered to look around as you were driving," Doug snapped, continuing to sprawl in the shade and not the least intimidated by the foreman's manner, "you'd have seen that we've done nearly twenty meters of new fence this morning."

"So, do another twenty." Karl had to shout to make himself heard over the idling motor of the truck. "When you're finished, reinforce the beams of that log cabin down by the creek. One more good windstorm and it'll be on the ground."

I could see Doug stiffen. It burned him the way Karl treated him like a raw hand, but he didn't say anything.

Karl revved up the truck motor, but almost immediately let it subside again. He turned to Gus and Billy. "Are either of you two guys planning to enter any of the events at Falkland?'' His voice had grown friendly, but there was an odd light in his eyes.

Gus and Billy shook their heads.

I glanced at Doug. He was watching Karl with a guarded, hostile expression.

"Not even the roping?" Karl went on. "That's one place where I figured you guys might be right up there with the best. Seems to me a lot of the top ropers on the rodeo circuit are native Indians." A funny note had crept into Karl's voice, and a muscle at one corner of his mouth had started to twitch.

Gus and Billy didn't answer. Neither did Doug.

I should have had enough sense to keep quiet, too, but instead I walked wide-eyed into the straight-man role that Karl had set up. "What makes roping any different from the other events?" I asked.

Karl gobbled my lead like a trout after a fat fly. "Because it only takes one hand." The obviously rehearsed words flowed out smugly and derisively, and though his lips were grinning his light-green eyes were hard and cold. "You don't think these guys would spend time practicing anything that needed both hands, do you? That'd leave them without one free for a handout." He roared with laughter at his own words.

I laughed, too.

Doug sure didn't. He got to his feet and glared at the foreman. "Why don't you get off these guys' backs for a change?" he demanded, his voice shaking with anger. "They're the best workers on the ranch. If you had half as much respect for wildlife and cattle and the environment as they do, the Circle Diamond would —''

Karl wasn't listening. He revved the truck motor once again, and still roaring with laughter, took off across the dry field.

To be honest, I couldn't understand why Doug was so mad. It had only been a joke, after all.

If I got the chance, I'd tell Hilary about it, I decided. I bet she'd think it was funny.

She was coming from the barn when we arrived in the ranch yard. She had been treating her horse for a strained tendon, and she must have been worried about him because when I first spotted her she was scowling. When she saw me, however, her whole face lit up and her eyes got a soft, dancing kind of look.

Even a person as hopeless with girls as I am can't ignore that sort of thing. I hurried over. I fell into step beside her and casually took hold of her hand.

When I realized what I had done I almost let go again, but she didn't seem to mind. In fact her fingers had managed to wrap themselves into mine, somehow.

I tightened my grip and grinned down at her.

For the next few minutes we walked in silence, just like Gus and Billy, I realized, and that reminded me about the joke. ''Old Karl has missed his calling,'' I began, still smiling. ''He should be doing a comedy routine at Las Vegas.'' I gave her a word-by-word replay of what had happened.

She must have still been worried about that horse she'd been treating, because she didn't even giggle. She just pulled her hand out of mine, said she'd forgotten something in the barn and took off.

"I'll wait for you," I called.

"No, thanks." She was gone.

It had happened so quickly I just stood there. What had I done wrong?

Two nights later she was at the barn again. She had her Arab gelding crosstied in the passageway and was polishing him as if he were made of fourteen-carat gold.

"Can I ask you something?" I said, coming up to her.

She went on brushing, but she didn't say no.

"Were you mad at me the other afternoon when I told you about Karl kidding Gus and Billy?"

"What d'you think?" She kept brushing, her eyes on the horse.

"But why?"

"If you can't see it yourself, there's no point in my trying to explain."

"Yes, there is. If you don't explain, how can I ever see?" She continued to polish her horse. "Things are different out here, you know." I felt all hot and embarrassed but I knew I had to try to make her understand. "If you were suddenly transported to the city there might be things you'd do wrong at first, too."

She stopped brushing and looked up. A thoughtful, half-puzzled look came into her eyes. "I never thought of that. Are things really different here?"

"Very."

She turned back to her horse. Again she started

brushing. But from the look of her back I could tell that she wasn't mad any more.

"Karl is always picking on Gus and Billy," Hilary said at last, "because they're Indian, and it isn't fair."

"He was just making a joke!"

Hilary shook his head. "He was dead serious. He's looking for a way to goad them into trouble so Dad will let them go."

I stared at her in surprise. "Why?"

"Karl doesn't judge people by the job they do or how hard they work. All he cares about is the color of their skin and their place on the social register." Her voice was bitter.

I looked down. There was a small pebble half buried in the ground by my right foot. I dug the toe of my runner under it till it was loose, then edged it back and forth a few inches. Hilary must have led a pretty sheltered life, I decided. "Half the people in the world feel the way Karl does," I told her. "There's no point in the other half getting all uptight and trying to change things. Doug should just relax. It isn't his funeral."

Her back tightened. The hand that a moment before had gently been brushing Sultan suddenly picked up speed.

Eager to fix things I rushed on: "I learned long ago that the only way to make it through life is to look after number one and close your eyes to what doesn't concern you. If you come across something you don't like, look the other way. That's what Doug should do."

The brushing grew more ferocious. In a cold, tight voice she said quietly, "Is that the most important thing in life, Tim? Looking out for number one?"

As she spoke she unsnapped the crossties and moved her horse toward the barn door. "I've gotta go," she mumbled, avoiding my eyes. "I want to put Sultan on the lunge line."

"Can I watch?"

"I'd rather you didn't. It distracts him when someone is there."

I doubted that. I'd seen her lunge Sultan lots of times when Doug or Mr. Brookes or one of the ranch hands was watching. But I couldn't force myself on her, and since I had nothing else to do I went to my room.

That was Wednesday.

Things went along that way for almost a week. Every time I tried to talk to Hilary she was busy doing something or going somewhere and didn't have time.

During the daytime it wasn't too bad, because I was busy all day mending fence with Doug and Gus and Billy. I could hardly believe it myself, but I was starting almost to enjoy it. I was even getting used to the business of having breakfast in the middle of the night. But the evenings were lonely.

I would sit in my room and think about what Hilary had said and what I had said and wonder where I had gone wrong. Whatever it was, I wished I could do something about it. I kept remembering that afternoon when we held hands. I could still feel the warm way she laced her fingers through mine and smiled up at me. She must have liked me at least a little bit. Then why . . .?

All week I sketched out imaginary scenes in my head. "I was hoping I'd see you," I would say when I accidentally bumped into her.

She would smile shyly. "Why?" she would ask.

"This is why," I would say, and take her hand. It'd be warm, maybe even trembling a little. This time when she laced her fingers through mine I'd . . .

But every time I tried to put my daydreams into action and arrange that accidental meeting, she took off before I had a chance to say a word.

Then suddenly, the next week, fate decided to take a hand.

As a rule the minute dinner was over in the evenings everybody scattered. Mrs. Brookes would disappear to her study to work on the book she was writing, Mr. Brookes would settle down to watch a ball game on TV, and Hilary and Doug would attend to some job or other. But one night as I headed into the living room to check the sports page of the *Ashcroft Journal* before joining Mr. Brookes and the ball game, everyone else came, too.

I looked around in surprise, wondering what was up. Then it occurred to me that it was July fifteenth, another payday, so maybe this was a family meeting. I started to leave.

"Don't go, Tim," Mr. Brookes urged as he started handing around some forms. "We're trying to get organized for the Falkland rodeo. The entry applications have to be in by this weekend."

I moved back into the living room. "What's everyone entering?" I asked.

"We won't know for sure till the end of the fifteenth round of *this* event," Mrs. Brookes replied,
looking at Hilary and Doug, who were deep in an
argument. Her eyes were twinkling. "Hilary
insists she's only going into the barrel races, but
Doug is trying to talk her into doing more. Doug,
on the other hand, is planning to enter practically
all the stadium events, and Hilary says he'll end
up hurting himself and should do less."

"What about you, Tim?" Mr. Brookes asked.
"Let's see if there's something you might like to
get into." As he spoke he scanned the list of
events.

I crossed my fingers. That was the last thing I
needed — to be in a rodeo.

Doug finished filling in his form, signed his
name at the bottom with a flourish and looked at
me. "How about the jousting?" he suggested with
a grin. "You're a pretty deadly horseman now
after all those lessons."

We'd gotten to be fairly good friends in the two
weeks I'd been helping repair fences, and I smiled
back at him.

Hilary laughed, but it wasn't a friendly
laugh — it was a hard, brittle one.

I went all cold inside, as if the sun had suddenly
been turned off. All at once the only thing that
mattered was finding a way to make Hilary
change her mind about me. Without even
stopping to think, I said deliberately, "I've
already entered. I got a form from Karl."

Mr. Brookes chuckled, an amused I-can-go-
along-with-a-joke gleam in his eyes. "Not the
grand melee, I hope," he said unconcernedly.

"I'd hate to send you back to your family all wrapped in bandages."

I met his glance without even the glimmer of a smile, not letting on that I didn't even know what the grand melee was. "No, sir. Just the regular jousting."

I glanced at Hilary. For the first time in days, instead of looking at me as if I had just crawled out from under a rock, she looked as if she really cared what happened to me.

But before she could speak, her mom was exclaiming in alarm, "You can't be serious, Tim!"

"If you'd seen him ride you wouldn't have to ask," Doug drawled in an amused tone. "Of course he's not serious."

Mrs. Brookes paid no attention. She was looking at her husband. "You told me when you got that letter from the committee that Karl wouldn't even encourage the hands to enter the jousting competition."

"And I agreed with him," Mr. Brookes replied. He turned to me. "The committee wrote asking us to support the jousting tournament by fielding a team. As a rule the Circle Diamond tries to take the lead in things like that, and I still feel guilty for backing down, but in this case, even though I knew it would reflect against the ranch, I couldn't ask the men to volunteer. It's just too dangerous."

I was beginning to feel uncomfortable. I hadn't expected Mr. or Mrs. Brookes to take any part in the discussion. I'd just tossed out my comment to get Hilary's attention. Then the plan had been to turn the thing into a joke, make her laugh and get back in her good books. Only somehow my joke had turned into a major issue. Now that Mr. and Mrs. Brookes had put their feelings on public display I couldn't turn around and say I was kidding, or Hilary would think I was deliberately making fun of them. How was that going to go over with someone who hadn't even thought Karl's joke was funny?

I started to sweat. I had to own up — as Doug had pointed out, nobody who rode the way I did could enter a jousting tournament and come out alive — only how was I going to do it? The minute I did the ice age would move in again, and this time it wouldn't only be Hilary who was freezing me out, it'd be her parents, too, and maybe even Doug.

Again I glanced at Hilary. The next second I was staring down at the rug, trying to look casual and hoping I wasn't blushing, because her face still wore that soft, caring expression.

I had to wait for the right moment, I told myself. After all, that was the secret of every successful operation. I would give people's feelings a chance to calm down a bit before explaining.

The Falkland rodeo was still two and a half weeks away. In two and a half weeks there'd be lots of chances for me to explain.

Six

As I said, the night I crowned myself big-mouth champion was July fifteenth, pay-day. As usual, all the hands were given the next few days off. Bright and early three days later everyone was back at work — except for Gus and Billy.

They had gone to Kamloops for their payday holiday and must have bumped into some of their friends and then somehow or other lost track of the days.

Mr. Brookes wasn't particularly upset. Apparently it happened occasionally with all the staff, and he took it in his stride. But Karl was livid. He made it sound as if Gus and Billy failed to show after every payday.

Actually, I couldn't see why Karl was so mad. It wasn't as if the ranch suffered. All that day when Gus and Billy didn't show, Doug imper-sonated a troop of Boy Scouts, doing their work and his own as well.

Karl, meantime, did nothing except pace back and forth like a fenced stallion. After lunch he hunted up Mr. Brookes, who'd come out with Doug and me to check on some yearling steers that were scheduled for market. As soon as the half ton came abreast of us, Karl started shouting his tale of misery.

"Every payday, Mr. Brookes!" he ended up. "What kind of employees are they? Let me hunt up a couple of reliable white boys to replace them."

"Are you sure white skins guarantee reliability?" Mr. Brookes asked dryly.

Karl flushed.

"You're being too hard on Gus and Billy. They're scarcely more than boys yet. Give them a chance to grow up. They'll learn responsibility."

"We can't afford to wait," Karl snapped. "There's no room for irresponsibility around a working ranch. It's too dangerous."

"True, but Gus and Billy aren't irresponsible when it comes to important things. Missing an occasional day's work after a holiday isn't that serious."

Karl didn't answer. He engaged the gears, popped the clutch and roared away, startling old Brownie with the noise he made.

Doug glared after him. "Gus and Billy are two of the best workers on the ranch. Lots of days they put in sixteen hours without a word of complaint, yet Karl would fire them for goofing off for a day."

"I don't agree with Karl any more than you do," Mr. Brookes replied, "but you have to remember he has a ranch to run. It's a business, not a resort hotel where people can turn up when they feel like it. The work doesn't take holidays."

"When Gus and Billy are away all their work gets taken care of, and Karl knows that."

Mr. Brookes chuckled. "That makes poor old Karl madder than ever. Thanks to your doing all the boys' work, he hasn't anything to complain about except the principle."

"Darn it all, Dad, it's only a couple of times a year that they come back late from holidays —"

"Would you settle for three or four?" Mr. Brookes amended, grinning. He kicked up his horse. "Come on. Let's finish with those yearlings before it gets any hotter."

Doug spurred his horse and caught up with his dad while I followed a little distance behind. Brownie wasn't in all that much of a hurry, and I had some thinking to do.

Would I have knocked myself out that way for Brad or Rory? I wondered. If one of them had goofed off on a job and the boss had been mad, would I have done their work for them? I had a sneaking suspicion that much as I liked them I wouldn't have bothered.

It was another whole day before Gus and Billy finally appeared. Then the way they set to work you couldn't help but forgive them. During the following three days they did more work than all the rest of the hands put together — including Karl.

Considering that the temperature was in the high thirties you have to hand it to them. I'd never worked in such heat. Granted it was dry, not humid like in Winnipeg — but thirty-eight degrees in the blazing sun is pretty hard to stand.

By Thursday I was exhausted. I decided if Gus and Billy could take a couple of days off and Mr.

Brookes had understood, then he would understand if I took off a couple of hours. So at noon when everybody else headed for lunch, I went to the barn. It was too hot to eat anyway, and I figured if I caught a couple of hours' sleep I might make it through the rest of the day.

As I let myself into the small corral that circled the barn I stopped for a minute to pat Mr. Brookes's favorite cutting horse, Gambler. Gambler was lame. He had shinsplints from running on the hard-baked ground.

That was the worst thing about the land in the Cariboo. It's a modified continuation of the California desert. In the summer there's not much rain, just day after day of cloudless sunshine, and by mid-July the clay soil gets as hard as a rock.

That's why Gambler was being kept in a confined space where the ground was soft. If he took it easy and didn't pound on those legs for a couple of weeks, they would heal and he would be fine. But, if he was let out of the barn enclosure and allowed to run on that hard-packed ground in the open country, he'd be lame for life.

But no one had explained that to poor old Gambler. He stood in the little corral gazing longingly into the hills where all the other horses were grazing.

"Take it easy, boy," I told him, rubbing his face. "You'll be back out there with your friends in a week or so. It won't be long." I knew just how he felt. At least he only had a few weeks to put in.

He nibbled my fingers, hoping I had a carrot or some oats, then limped away a few steps.

I continued across the small corral, swung the sliding wooden barn door open just far enough so I could squeeze through, closed it behind me and scrambled up the ladder to the hayloft to sleep for a while.

I slept longer than I planned. It was more than two hours before I finally woke up. I tore out of there in such a hurry I didn't even bother with the ladder rungs. I just held onto the top one and jumped, then I ran out the barn door and across the small corral.

Gambler looked at me expecting another rub, but I didn't stop. I slid the wooden tongue back on the swinging pole gate, ran through, gave the gate a mighty shove to swing it closed behind me and took off for the far pasture where I was supposed to be helping mend fence.

I was in luck. Everyone else was late getting back, too. Doug had been in the office with his dad. The plan was that as soon as he was ready, he'd take over tabulating the ranch accounts, so a couple of times each month he and his dad went over things together. There must have been more to discuss than usual today, because he only arrived back on the fence line about five minutes before I did. As for Gus and Billy, they were approaching from the other direction as I ran up.

To make up for lost time we worked extra hard for the next couple of hours.

Along about four o'clock the half ton chugged to a stop beside us. "Good work, boys." Karl's voice was heavy with sarcasm. "I've got to hand it to you. This time you've really fixed things."

Doug glanced up. But instead of giving Karl the

satisfaction of asking what he meant, he just grunted and returned his attention to pivoting the posthole digger another turn into the dry earth.

"Maybe it would have been better if those two friends of yours hadn't come back from their pay-day holiday at all," Karl went on.

Doug couldn't keep quiet any longer. "Either make sense or leave us alone so we can get some work done," he snapped.

"Does ten thousand bucks make sense to you?" Karl said bitingly. "I hope so, because that's what it's cost the ranch to have your two buddies come to work today. Five g's apiece, unless you figure it should be a three-way split."

Doug stopped pivoting the auger.

"I guess if you all chip in," Karl continued, pretending to be working something out in his head, "about three months' pay apiece should fix things."

Doug's face darkened with impatience. "Okay. You've had your fun. Now tell us what we're sup-posed to have done."

"Not you — them." Karl jabbed a thumb in the direction of the two ranch hands. "They left the gate of the small corral open and your dad's cutting horse is long gone, shinsplints and all. By the time we find him way off in those sunbaked hills he'll be so lame he'll never be any use."

"Gambler?" Doug's face had paled.

"Gambler."

A dull, sick feeling settled in the pit of my stomach. I was picturing Gambler standing in the small corral gazing forlornly into the hills. I was seeing myself rushing past him, opening the gate, shoving it closed behind me but not stopping to make sure it was shut.

"What makes you think Gus and Billy were anywhere near the barn or the small corral?" Doug challenged. His chin was raised and he was staring hard into Karl's eyes.

A smug grin came over Karl's face. "This," he answered. He held out a package of cigarettes.

Doug looked quickly at Billy. He was the only person on the ranch who smoked menthols.

I'd seen those cigarettes in the loft when I'd been there at lunchtime. I'd meant to take them with me when I left and give them to Billy, only when I woke I was in such a hurry I forgot.

Doug was looking at Billy with a guarded expression. "Were you up in the hayloft at noon?"

Billy shook his head. "Not today." His voice was low. "I left those cigarettes up there a couple of days ago. I meant to go back for them."

"What were you doing with cigarettes in the hayloft anyway?" Karl demanded. "Deliberately trying to set the place on fire?"

Billy colored but he didn't answer. He knew as well as the rest of us that it was a rule never to smoke in a hay barn.

"D'you two make a habit of going up to the loft for a smoke?" Karl continued in the same sarcastic tone. He sounded like the prosecuting attorney in a B-grade made-for-TV movie.

Billy's flush deepened. "We weren't smoking. I took the package of cigarettes out of my pocket when I stretched out so I wouldn't squash it."

"I'll bet!" Revving up the truck motor, Karl

took off, purposely covering us with a cloud of thick, dry dust.

There was silence for a minute. Then in a quiet, even voice Doug said, "You really weren't anywhere near the barn at lunchtime?"

"We weren't. Honest."

"Then why didn't you tell Karl where you were?"

"It would have made him even madder."

"Why?"

"It was so hot we went back to the bunkhouse to finish off the last couple of beer left over from payday."

Doug let out his breath in a long, slow sigh. "Great. The one time we need to be able to say where you were so we can prove you weren't in the barn, you have to be breaking the rules and drinking beer in the bunkhouse. Now what do we do?"

The two ranch hands were silent.

"There's not much chance that whoever really did leave that gate open is going to ride up on a white horse and admit it," Doug went on. "Not with Dad waiting to string him up by his thumbs to the nearest tree." He kicked at the log on the ground in front of him. "The important thing right now is to try to find poor old Gambler. Come on." He set off at a run for the barn.

Gus and Billy hurried after him.

I felt too awful to follow. Why hadn't I realized how easy it would be for a horse to nudge a gate open when it moved outward like that one did, rather than inward? Why hadn't I taken the time to make sure it was firmly closed? Gambler must have pushed up against it in his yearning to be out with his friends, and felt it move. For a horse as smart as Gambler, that's all the invitation he'd need.

I sat down beside the fence and dug my heels into the dirt. I probably should tell Mr. Brookes, but what would be the point? The horse was gone and probably lame for life by this time. Saying that I'd goofed about the gate wasn't going to change that; it would just get me in more trouble. And what would that do to Mom and Dad? After sending me out to visit their friends for the summer, how would they feel if they discovered I had cost Mr. Brookes ten thousand dollars?

I looked toward the barn in the distance. Doug and Gus and Billy had almost reached it. In a minute they'd have their horses saddled and they'd be heading into the hills.

I pushed my heels farther into the ground. Was it ever hard. Poor old Gambler. I hoped they found him quickly.

Seven

*A*t about ten o'clock that night the guys came back with Gambler.

Obviously, cutting horses aren't priced in five figures for nothing, and Gambler must be even smarter than most. He must have felt just the way Mr. Brookes did about getting himself lamed for life, because he'd meandered less than a mile into the hills to a peaceful spot where the grass was tasty and stayed there. Apparently when the guys spotted him and moved toward him, he didn't even budge. He just waited for Doug to put a rope around his neck and lead him home again.

I felt really good when I heard that because it proved I had been right not to say anything. Gambler was safe, no harm had been done and I hadn't ended up in anybody's bad books. If I'd made a big thing about it and owned up, Mr. Brookes might have been mad enough to send me home. Two weeks ago I'd have welcomed that, but not now — not when Hilary was just beginning to warm up to me again. Besides, I was kind of enjoying myself. I was even starting to develop a few muscles.

Next morning when I went down to breakfast I was really feeling great. I figured everybody else on the ranch would be feeling great, too, but Doug and Mr. Brookes were facing each other over the dining-room table like fighting cocks squaring off for a bout.

"After that business with Gambler yesterday, I'm putting Gus and Billy directly under Karl's supervision," Mr. Brookes was saying as I walked in. He gave me a curt nod of greeting, then returned his attention to Doug.

"Dad, you can't! Karl hates Gus and Billy. He'll make their lives so miserable they'll have no option but to quit."

"I can't help that, son. You know I like Gus and Billy, and I've tried to be lenient with them. I haven't even minded when they've missed a couple of days' work now and then. But not only were they irresponsible about Gambler, they also broke the cardinal rule around here and took cigarettes into the barn."

"But they weren't smoking, Dad! Billy tried to explain that to Karl. A couple of days ago they went into the barn where it was cool to take a breather, and Billy took his cigarette package out of his pocket so he wouldn't lie on it. As for the gate being left open yesterday, I don't know who was responsible, but it wasn't Gus or Billy. They were nowhere near the barn."

"How do you know?"

"They gave me their word."

The expression on Mr. Brookes's face continued to be stern. "Unfortunately, their word isn't enough. It would be different if someone could vouch for the fact that they were busy somewhere else, but no one saw them." He helped himself to a slice of ham from the platter in front of him. "I'm sorry, but till Billy and Gus show a little more responsibility, I want them to report to Karl first thing each morning and work directly under his supervision." He held out the ham platter.

Doug passed it on without even glancing at it. "I'm not hungry," he muttered. Shoving his untouched eggs away, he got to his feet and strode out of the room, his heels making a muted staccato rhythm on the carpeted floor.

I felt tight and funny inside. "Mr. Brookes," I began.

"Not right now, Tim, if you don't mind." His voice was curt. Leaving his own breakfast untouched, he also strode out of the room.

I put some ketchup on my eggs, then helped myself to the ham. It's my favorite breakfast — particularly when the ham is warm and the eggs are crispy around the edges. I picked up a big forkful, but then put it down untouched. I wasn't hungry, either.

Next day was Saturday. As a rule Karl takes it easy on Saturday and Sunday. He does his own thing and leaves the work to the rest of the ranch hands. But not this weekend. He had Billy and Gus wrapped up like disobedient puppies, ordering them around every minute.

I could see the anger starting to build in Billy's eyes. He's not as easygoing as Gus, and he hasn't got Gus's control. As the hours passed the resentment continued to build. I knew before much longer the top would blow off, Billy would do something dumb. Gus would stand up for him and they'd both be sacked.

I felt a needle stab of guilt. If it hadn't been for the Gambler business they wouldn't be chained to Karl like slaves to an overseer.

The very next minute I realized that wasn't true. The Gambler business was incidental. The real problem was that Karl didn't like them. Sooner or later he was going to find a way to fire them — if not because of Gambler, then for the next thing that came along — and that had nothing to do with me. If they hadn't been late coming back from payday Karl probably wouldn't have been half as mad in the first place.

The way they were behaving right now wasn't my fault, either. Instead of going all surly and hostile and making Karl even madder, why didn't they just coast along till things blew over?

Dinner that Saturday evening was a pretty glum affair. Gus and Billy didn't appear at all. Neither did Karl. Doug reminded me of an unexploded shell that had been left sitting dangerously close to a bonfire, and Mr. Brookes was withdrawn and silent.

The stew went down in absolute silence. Halfway through the apple pie, Doug looked up. "You can't let things go on like this, Dad. Karl's treating Billy and Gus like a pair of convicts. The reason they're not here for dinner is that he's stuck them with extra work. By the time they're through everything will be cold."

"I'll ask the cook to keep things hot for them," Mr. Brookes replied. His expression softened. "I feel as badly about this as you do, Doug. I appreciate how tough it is for them to make a success of a job in a non-Indian society. But I have no patience with people who turn and run. If you do something wrong, own up to it and take the consequences. Until Billy and Gus prove to me that they are mature enough to accept the responsibility for their actions, they'll have to continue to be supervised.

"But they weren't responsible! They weren't in the barn!"

Mr. Brookes looked intently into Doug's face. "Are you sure?"

"I'm dead sure."

I waited for him to go on and tell his dad about the beer-drinking in the bunkhouse, but he didn't. He must have decided that adding that item to the irresponsibility scoreboard wasn't going to help. But the sincerity in his voice impressed his father.

"I agree that carelessness isn't typical of Gus and Billy," Mr. Brookes said slowly, "particularly where livestock are concerned. They have a real feeling for animals." The hint of a smile pulled at his lips. "I was afraid when Gambler first went lame that he was going to end up half a ton overweight, the way Gus and Billy were always stopping by the small corral with a handful of oats for him. Suppose I discuss it with Karl again? Perhaps we've both jumped to conclusions. Maybe after thinking it over he'll agree that he could be wrong about Gambler —".

"Fat chance!" Doug retorted. "Karl won't think anything over except how to fire Gus and Billy."

Mr. Brookes's expression tightened once again. "If you're going to accuse Karl of having tunnel vision, make sure you aren't being equally narrow-minded yourself. Don't forget there are two sides to everything. Maybe Karl has some justification for his opinion. If Gus and Billy really cared about the ranch —"

"They do care, Dad! Honest they do. You should hear them in town on a night off. They just don't say much around here, that's all."

"I'm not saying I don't believe you, but I'd like to have some proof. I agree they work hard, but they get paid good money to do so. What have they ever done that is extra?"

It was Doug's turn to be thoughtful. For a long moment he returned his dad's look without speaking, then a considering glint came into his eyes. "Suppose," he said thoughtfully as if weighing something in his mind as he spoke, "we could find some way to show that Gus and Billy do care about the ranch — that they're willing to put their efforts where their mouths are. Would that change your mind?"

"Yes, if at the same time you could provide me with reasonable proof that they weren't the ones responsible for leaving the corral gate unfastened."

Doug nodded slowly. He pushed back his chair, got to his feet and, with that considering expression still creasing his face, he left the room.

Obviously he had some plan, but what? I wondered.

My wildest imaginings didn't come even close to the answer.

Eight

"**E**xactly one week, Sir Timothy," Doug greeted me at the breakfast table next morning. "This time next week the Falkland rodeo will be in full swing, with you as a featured performer in the sporting event of the century — the medieval joust."

I forced a grin but I wasn't amused. With all the worry about Gambler and Gus and Billy I hadn't had a chance yet to tell Hilary and her parents that my jousting talk had been a joke. But darn it all, if Doug kept playing it up I'd never find the right moment.

"Don't you think you should be practicing?" Doug went on as if he didn't know perfectly well that I hadn't the slightest intention of having anything to do with the exercise. "You don't want to get hurt. Since it's Sunday and there aren't too many chores to do, why don't we go down to the barn after breakfast and I'll run over some of the things you should know."

All at once it occurred to me that he wasn't joking, that he really meant that bit about practicing. I stared at him in confusion. Why? Surely he knew I hadn't sent in any entry form. He'd said right out that anybody who rode the way I did —

"Yes, by all means take Tim in hand." Mr. Brookes's voice broke into my thoughts. He turned to me. "You've got to know what you're doing, or as Doug says you could be hurt. If you really want to try it, I suppose one or two passes won't be too serious. But to be honest, I wish we could talk you out of jousting."

I forgot all about Doug, because this was exactly the chance I'd been waiting for. Now I knew how Noah must have felt when the rains stopped and the sun came bursting through. Not only could I get out of the hole I'd dug for myself without having to admit that I'd never had any intention of jousting, but I could win some Brownie points at the same time. All I had to do was adopt an unselfish, long-suffering tone, then reluctantly agree for their sakes to give up the jousting. "If you really think . . ." I began, trying to sound disappointed.

"I'll come down to the barn and help with the lessons," Hilary interrupted, seemingly unaware that I had been speaking. She pushed back her chair. "I've got to put a coat of saddle soap on the boots I want to wear for the barrels, but as soon as I've done that I'll join you." And without waiting for an answer, she jumped up from the table and ran from the room.

There was a smile on Mr. Brookes's face as he watched her. "Not interrupting when other people are speaking seems to be one of the things Hilary hasn't learned yet. Sorry, Tim. What were you starting to say?"

The forty days weren't over after all. I reached for the cereal bowl and poured myself a large helping that I didn't want, but it gave me something to look at so I wouldn't have to meet Mr. Brookes's gaze. "Nothing important," I replied, trying to sound casual. "Just that if you really think I should practice, then okay, I'll go with Doug after breakfast."

I could feel Doug's eyes on me. I didn't want to look at him, either, so I bent over my bowl and began shoveling in the granola as if I hadn't seen food for a week.

Doug waited till I was finished, then we left the house.

As we stepped into the yard, Gus and Billy appeared out of nowhere and joined us. I was surprised. I'd thought Karl would have had them jumping to his orders all day. My surprise must have showed, because Doug said simply, "Dad told Karl to give them the day off."

We headed for the barn. Halfway there Doug stopped. "I've got a favor to ask," he said quietly, a thoughtful, measuring expression in his eyes.

I felt a nag of premonition. What could I do for Doug Brookes that he couldn't do a hundred times better for himself? I tried to look unconcerned and waited.

"Remember that letter Dad was talking about the other night from the rodeo committee?" He took a folded letter out of his shirt pocket and handed it to me.

I read it through quickly. The gist was that the rodeo committee had put up a lot of cash to get an official international jousting tournament included in the annual Falkland rodeo. They'd done it because the local ranchers had asked them to. Now, however, it seemed that the ranchers weren't getting involved, and the committee, which had put up the money, was about to take a bath. They were writing to ask each of the major ranches in the area to field a four-member team that would compete in the full roster of jousting events. The winning team would get a trophy, a small cash prize and the satisfaction of knowing it had helped save the rodeo from maybe going under.

When I got to the end of the letter I read it again, more carefully this time. It still didn't seem to register.

"Since you're already entered as an individual competitor in the jousting," Doug said without even a trace of embarrassment at the obvious lie, "we wondered if you'd also ride as fourth member of the Circle Diamond jousting team."

I was stunned. "I can barely ride! I'd be killed!"

"Don't be melodramatic. You're already planning to joust, so why the panic? The team events won't be all that much more dangerous than the individual contests."

I knew I was staring at him like a six-year-old, but I couldn't help it. All I could think of was how he could make such a statement with a straight face when he knew I hadn't the slightest intention of jousting in any kind of event.

I looked sideways at Gus and Billy. I didn't want to lose face in front of them. The news that I was planning to joust had brought their first looks of respect, and it felt good.

But not good enough to justify suicide.

I turned back to Doug, casting about frantically for a way out. 'You can't ride on a jousting team,'' I argued. "You've signed up for just about all the rodeo events. You won't have time to —''

"I've withdrawn from the other events because this is more important. Our ranch is one of the oldest and most respected in the area. If we support the jousting tournament, the other ranches will follow our lead. If we don't, neither will they. That's what Dad was hinting at the other night when he said he felt guilty about backing down. It's also why Billy and Gus and I have decided to enter a Circle Diamond team, only we need a fourth rider.''

I stared at him in disbelief. He couldn't be serious!

"Please, Tim. It's not only for the ranch; it's for Gus and Billy, too. This is our chance to prove to Dad and Karl that Gus and Billy aren't just interested in themselves — that they're willing to risk their necks for the ranch's reputation.''

It was a minute before I could speak at all, then I managed to say, "Anybody on the ranch would be better than me. The only thing you'd win with me on the team is a bunch of jeers.''

"Maybe, but nobody else wants to join.''

"Why not?''

"It's too dangerous.''

If I hadn't been still reeling from shock I'd have laughed. Team jousting was too dangerous for guys who'd been brought up on horseback, and they wanted me to do it!

I shook my head. "It's not that I'm chicken," I said, which of course wasn't true, "but there'd be no point in it. How're you gonna win any respect for the ranch or for Gus and Billy if the team gets laughed out of the arena?"

I could feel three pairs of eyes watching me as I headed back to the ranch house, but I kept going. What I'd said was true, and after they'd had a chance to think about it for a bit they'd see that. In fact, before the day was over they'd be thanking me for refusing, because someone else was sure to offer to ride with them, and then they'd have a team that could win the respect they were after.

Nine

During my first week at the Circle Diamond, after I'd messed up on the haying, I had been initiated into the world of being ignored. But that had been nothing to what I experienced during the next two days. If you've ever played that childhood game of isolation you'll understand. Doug and Gus and Billy behaved as if I simply didn't exist. They looked right through me.

On Monday morning when Karl took Gus and Billy off to finish repairing the fence by the big alfalfa field, Doug went with them. I tagged along. While Billy and Gus and Doug dug postholes, Karl shouted and found fault. I stood in the background and watched.

It was still as hot as it had been all the previous week, so after a while I offered to spell the others off so they could have a breather. I might as well have been talking in a vacuum. No one even seemed to hear me.

During my month on the ranch I had discovered that haying and building fences and moving irrigation pipes are hard work, but that Monday I discovered something even harder — standing around watching while everybody else works.

On Tuesday I stayed in my room. I sent word down in the morning that I wasn't feeling well. Immediately Mrs. Brookes was up with a thermometer and solicitous looks, but I told her I just had a headache. I pretended I was sleepy.

"It's working in this heat when you're not used to it," she told me. "You just stay where you are. I'll send some soup up at noon. By this afternoon you'll be feeling much better."

"Yes, ma'am. Thank you," I said.

After she left I tried to go back to sleep. In Winnipeg I would have been sleeping till about eleven every morning. Why couldn't I sleep here?

I finally gave it up and got dressed and started a letter home.

I hadn't written very often. I just couldn't seem to think of things I figured my family would be interested in. Maybe I could tell them about the jousting tournament, only I didn't want to. Thinking about the tournament made me uncomfortable.

I pushed the paper away and chewed on the end of my ballpoint.

"Where in the Sam Hill do you two misfits think you're going?" Karl's raspy voice floated up to me from the yard outside.

I put down my pen and moved toward the window. Karl, Billy and Gus were directly below.

"Refilling the baler," Gus replied. He held up a roll of baler twine. "The south meadow is raked and dried. Doug said we'd start to bale it tomorrow."

"I wouldn't trust you guys to tie up a Christmas parcel," Karl yelled, grabbing the roll of twine. "You'd probably try to lock in the new roll with the motor running."

"Come on, Karl," Billy protested. "You know darn well we've done it hundreds of times."

"Well, you're not doing it the hundred and first. Not as long as I'm foreman on this ranch. I'll get one of the other guys to do it so I'll know it's been done right." With the roll of twine still in his hands, Karl strode away.

Did he ever know how to make a guy feel small. I was sure glad it was Gus and Billy he was mad at and not me. If they were smart they'd make sure not to rile him any more.

But Billy, especially, seemed to be programmed on a destruction course. As Karl moved toward the barn, Billy took a step toward him. If Gus hadn't grabbed his arm he'd have caught Karl a dandy.

"Smarten up," Gus snarled in an undertone as soon as Karl was safely out of earshot. "Do you want to get fired?"

"It'd be better than this."

"How d'you expect to get a job anywhere else if Karl spreads the word that you hit him?"

Billy's shoulders slumped like a balloon that someone had just let the air out of. He scuffed the toe of his boot into the dusty ground. "What difference is it going to make in the long run? Sooner or later Karl is going to find a way to get us fired, and there's no way he'll ever give us a recommendation anyway."

"Mr. Brookes will. Or Doug."

"What good will that do if Karl spreads all kinds of lies about us first?"

All of a sudden it wasn't Billy talking, it was my friend Rory. A couple of years ago Rory got himself into trouble for smoking pot at school. Ever since then every time there was any kind of trouble Rory was called in and made to prove his innocence. Just before the end of term it had happened again.

The janitor had found some grass in the washroom. I was sitting next to Rory in English class when the announcement came over the loudspeaker saying that he was to report to the office.

"Don't tell me they think you had anything to do with that," I told him.

"They think I have something to do with everything," Rory replied. His voice was bitter. "Maybe other people are innocent till they're proved guilty, but I'm sure not. No matter what the problem is, I'm suspect number one."

I looked into the yard. Billy and Gus were moving in the direction of the alfalfa field where Doug had started up the raker. They were walking with about as much enthusiasm as if they'd been conscripted to be the first cleanup men at Chernobyl after the accident.

I watched till they were out of sight.

Mrs. Brookes had been wrong, I reflected. Staying in my room hadn't made me feel better. Now I really felt sick.

Ten

On Wednesday I got up at five-thirty as usual and went down for breakfast.

"Feeling better?" Mr. Brookes greeted me.

"Yes, thanks."

Doug looked through me as he'd been doing for the past two days, then pushed his plate away and got up from the table.

"There's no need to be in that much of a hurry," Mr. Brookes told him. "Sit down and enjoy your breakfast."

"I've got a lot of work to do," Doug muttered, reaching for the rumpled Stetson he'd left on the table by the door.

"What are you doing today?"

"Starting to bale the south meadow."

"I'll help," I said. I moved after him.

"Have your breakfast first," Mr. Brookes said.

"Thanks, but I'm not hungry." It was a lie. I was famished. I'd hardly eaten a thing yesterday because I'd felt too rotten, but there were more important things to do at the moment than worry about my stomach. I grabbed my hat from the same table where Doug's had been sitting and opened the door.

Doug was halfway across the yard on his way to the barn.

"What horse do I practice on — Trouble?" I called.

He stopped. He turned around slowly and just looked at me.

"I said, what horse do I practice on, Sir Douglas?"

A slow smile broke over his face. "You'll do it?" he asked unbelievingly.

"I'll regret it, but I'll do it."

Everyone should play isolation for the sheer enjoyment of seeing that first smile when you come out of it. It's like the sun breaking through the fog.

Doug was grinning like a six-year-old at a birthday party. "It'll take us about four hours to bale that hay, then we'll all learn to joust. Come on." He started jogging toward the bunkhouse.

"Gus! Billy!" he shouted as he spotted the two coming across the yard. "Sir Timothy is going to play out his option after all. We'll be the best jousting team in the history of show business."

It didn't take long to do the baling. In fact I've never seen anyone work so fast. Then we hightailed it back to the barn.

"There's really nothing to this jousting business," Doug explained. "It's exactly like the old medieval tournaments, except that instead of killing your opponent as they did in the fourteenth century, you're just supposed to unseat him."

I wasn't too sure it wouldn't amount to the same thing.

"All we expect you to do, Tim," Doug went on, "is to keep your horse in tight alongside the tilt. It doesn't matter whether you unseat your opponent or not, just so long as you meet him. Billy and Gus and I will build up the points for the team."

I nodded. It sounded easy enough.

"When you fall off," he said, as an afterthought, "remember to yell."

I'd forgotten about the falling off part. "So the stretcher bearers will come for me," I asked, "or just to let the public know that I am about to die?"

"To get the air out of your lungs, lamebrain. And keep yelling until you hit the ground. If you'd done that a few weeks ago when you came off old Trouble you wouldn't have been gasping like a landed fish."

"If this is going to be anything like riding old Trouble —" I began.

"It won't be," Gus assured me quickly. "This won't even hurt."

I looked at him and grinned. Not because I believed him. There was no way I was going to believe that being knocked off a galloping horse wasn't going to hurt. I grinned because it was nice to feel we were all in this together.

"Besides, it may not be you who gets knocked off," Billy put in. "If you make sure you catch the other guy's shield right in the center, he'll be the one to take the nosedive.''

I had a sudden picture of Sir Timothy felling his armed opponent with one mighty blow of his lance. Maybe I was going to manage to carry off this jousting thing after all. "Start at the beginning and give me the full drill," I said, "rules, no-no's, everything.''

"You've seen a joust, haven't you?" Doug asked.

I shook my head.

"You're right. We'd better start at the beginning.''

He did. He explained that there were six or seven different types of contests in modern jousting competitions, but the one that mattered, the one that divided the men from the boys, was the joust itself — mounted combat with lances and shields.

Two knights lined up at opposite ends of a field, on opposite sides of a chest-high wooden fence, called a tilt, which ran lengthwise down the field. Each held a four-meter lance in one hand and a shield in the other.

The moment the bugle sounded to announce the beginning of the contest, the knights would gallop toward each other. When they met, each one would try to hit the other's shield and send him flying.

"If you knock the other fellow off, you win four points," Doug explained. "If he stays in the saddle but you succeed in striking his shield, you score two. And if it happens the other way he gets the points.''

"What happens if he misses your shield and hits you somewhere else?" The possibility was worrying me. "Could that happen?"

"Uh-huh."

"Does he get anything for that?"

"Ten years if he runs you clean through," Doug answered, grinning.

"No, seriously. Does he get anything?"

"He doesn't get any actual points, but I guess you could say he gets some psychological ones."

"How?" Even to my ears my voice sounded hollow.

"That sort of thing has a tendency to cut down on the number of contestants in the rest of the events."

Doug, Billy and Gus were all smiling delightedly, but I wasn't sure it was a joke.

All afternoon we practiced. The others were pretty impressive. I couldn't manage to keep old Brownie close enough to the tilt to take any part in the action.

The decision that I should stick with Brownie had been unanimous. By no stretch of the imagination could she be considered an outstanding ranch pony, but I had mastered the art of staying on her back. That seemed to be the most important issue.

It would have been nice if she'd been more enthusiastic about jousting, but maybe she'd tried it before. The minute she saw Gus or Doug or Billy galloping down the opposite side of the makeshift tilt we'd erected, with a lance pointing straight at her, she decided she didn't want to play. She simply moved at right angles away from the line we were supposed to be riding.

"We could blindfold her," Billy suggested. Thank goodness he was only kidding.

"Or tie that inside rein down to hold her head in," Gus suggested.

But Doug opted for leaving it for today and trying some of the other contests instead.

"I hope they're easier," I muttered.

"They're a cinch," he assured me.

First we had a go at the half-lance relay. It's a standard relay race. The teams line up and the first rider of each team does a four-hundred-meter gallop around the tilt and back again, carrying a half-lance. He hands it off to his teammate, who does the same, and so on. It was decided we'd put me third. That way Gus and Billy could build up a good initial lead for our team, then Doug could try to get it back again after I'd blown it.

"The next one takes a little more know-how," Doug said as we were giving our horses a breather after three runs through the relay. "It's the wench rescue race." He grinned. "Tomorrow we'll get Hilary to volunteer to be the wench, but for today we'll just go over the course."

He dismounted and picked up a stick. "Have you ever watched a barrel race?" he asked, looking at me.

I shook my head.

"Then I'd better draw the course. If you take the wrong direction you're out."

With the point of the stick he made three small holes in the ground like a cloverleaf — one at twelve o'clock, one at three o'clock and one at nine o'clock. Just under the twelve he drew a large X.

"You start here," he said, poking his stick in at

six o'clock. "Head for nine o'clock and go around the barrel. Make sure you go inside it first, around the back, then circle outside and around the front. Don't go outside first." He traced the pattern in the dirt. "Then go across to three o'clock. Here you go clockwise around the barrel and back into the middle of the clock, then head toward twelve o'clock."

His stick stopped at the big X.

"What's that?" I asked.

"A beautiful girl tied to a stake. You dismount, leaving your horse standing, and untie her. Remount, swing her up in front of you and continue to the twelve o'clock barrel. Circle it the same as the others then gallop straight to six o'clock."

"Fastest time wins?"

"Fastest time wins eight points, second six and third four."

"What happens when you let go of the reins to untie the girl and your horse decides he's had enough and heads off?"

"You lose points. But he won't. Not if you let your reins dangle. He'll stand."

"Even old Brownie?"

Doug nodded. "Just one thing," he added. "I hope you have a strong regard for the fair sex and that your sense of chivalry is polished and bright, because this is a case of ladies first. It doesn't matter what else you do wrong, but don't lose your wench. If you do, the whole team will be disqualified."

The next contest we went over was the dagger swoop. A large wheel is mounted upright on a post. The wheel has daggers stuck into it, and the point of the game is to gallop down a track as the wheel is spinning, seize a dagger, gallop back and place the dagger in the waiting hand of the Grand Knight Marshal. Since we didn't have the equipment, Doug just explained that one; we didn't try it.

"Fastest time wins ten points," he said.

"Hardly seems sufficient incentive to risk losing an arm."

He grinned. "No one ever loses an arm. A little dignity, maybe, but that's all."

"Run that by me again?"

"Some of those daggers are easy to get out, but sometimes you reach for one that isn't. If that happens, forget it. Otherwise you'll be going around on the wheel, too."

I think I must have paled a little because they all laughed. "D'you think there's much chance that we'll have to do that one?"

"Probably not, but you've got to know about it just in case."

The next two races Doug described sounded fairly straightforward. One was called pig sticking, the other ringing. The first involved dislodging sticks, called "pigs," with the point of the rider's lance as he galloped past; the other involved scooping up rings. In either game the worst thing that could happen was that I'd miss everything and get laughed at, but laughter was painless.

"The final event, of course, will be the grand melee," Doug finished. He tried to sound casual, but he failed.

I felt another pang of premonition. That was the one Mr. Brookes had joked about that first night. "Break it to me gently," I managed.

"All the knights on one team line up and face all the knights on the other."

"On foot?" I asked hopefully.

"On horseback. At a signal from the Grand Knight Marshal they gallop toward each other and each tries to wrestle one of the others to the ground."

"One against one?"

"To start. But as soon as one knight throws his opponent he's free to go to the help of any of his team members."

"So maybe in the end it could be four to one?"

"Could be."

There was something about the sound of that I didn't like.

"Are we armed?" I asked.

Doug shook his head. "No weapons. Just brute force. But don't worry about it. It's clearly stated in the rules for the grand melee that the moment a knight feels his opponent coming out of the saddle he's honor bound to help support him as he falls so he won't hit the ground too hard."

"What if everyone hasn't read the rules?"

Doug grinned. "By Saturday we'll have shaped you into the greatest jouster in history. You haven't a thing to worry about."

I had an idea he meant jester. What could I possibly learn in three short days except what an idiot I was?

Eleven

By dinnertime that night the news had spread all over the ranch that the Circle Diamond was entering a team in the jousting tournament at Falkland. Since Mr. Brookes had said earlier that he wasn't going to ask the ranch hands to volunteer to make up a team because jousting was too dangerous, there was considerable amazement. What kamikaze types were eager enough to risk their necks for the Circle Diamond's reputation?

Before long everyone knew that Doug was involved, but who the other team members were was a closely kept secret. Doug had planned it that way. The moment we entered the dining room the questions started. Doug fielded them carefully without giving any information. I just kept my mouth shut.

When Karl came in he reached for the big platter of pork chops, filled his plate and looked over at Doug. "Is it true, this nonsense I hear about a Circle Diamond jousting team?"

"It's true," Doug replied. His voice was friendly. I wondered what was coming next. "You know the committee is really worried about losing a pile of money if the jousting tournament falls flat. They wrote us specially asking for support. I guess they knew if the Circle Diamond supported them the other ranches would, too."

"You're crazy!" Karl snapped. "Jousting is insane."

"Will you ride with us, Karl?" Doug asked. "We could sure use you."

"Fat chance! How many men have you got lined up so far?"

"For starters, Tim and me, then —"

"Tim!" Karl's voice was heavy with sarcasm. "Trying to get rid of him?"

I felt a little hurt. I didn't think I was that hopeless. "I offered," I put in quickly.

"Then unoffer," Karl retorted. "You'll only end up hurting yourself. Maybe seriously."

"How about it, Karl?" Doug urged again. "Will you ride with us? We need good men, and you're the best horseman on the ranch."

"You don't need good riders, you need daredevils."

"Well, you're a pretty brave guy —"

"Brave, maybe, but not crazy. I wouldn't be caught dead having any part of this nonsense. Jousting is the most harebrained sport ever invented. I don't care how hard the rodeo committee begs for support. It's their own fault if they're in trouble — they should have known better than to get involved in anything so stupid."

"If we field a team, most of the other ranches will, too," Doug pointed out.

"Then the other ranches are dumber than I thought."

There was silence for a moment. "I guess you're right," Doug said at last. "Jousting is pretty dangerous. How do you figure it got to be so popular back in the Middle Ages?"

"Obviously people back then were too stupid to think up a game where everyone didn't end up getting killed."

"D'you think many people actually got hurt?"

"Are you kidding? Go back to school and read your history books."

"But it's a lot safer now, isn't it?"

"You call it safe to let a bunch of hotheads go charging at each other with lances in their hands?"

"The lances aren't all that sharp —"

"The fact that they're lances is enough. And falling off a galloping horse doesn't tickle."

All this time Mr. Brookes had been sitting at his end of the table playing with his food. He was just listening, a half smile on his lips.

"Then do you figure," Doug was saying, studying Karl's face thoughtfully, "if it's that dangerous, that we should just withdraw the ranch entry?"

"You can't withdraw now!" Karl stormed. "You'd make the whole bunch of us look like sissies." He stabbed a pork chop with his fork. "That's the trouble with you young punks. It never occurs to you to think before you rush into something. You should have thought about how dangerous it was before you sent in that entry form. Now that you've done it, you've got to stick to it."

Doug continued to frown thoughtfully. Then in a slow voice he admitted, "You're right. Having gone this far we've got to field a Circle Diamond team. We can't pull out without making the ranch look ridiculous." His glance traveled the length of the table. "So, come on, you guys. You heard what Karl said. Who's willing to take a few bumps in order to defend the Circle Diamond's honor?"

It seemed that everyone's pork chops suddenly required a lot of attention. Every head was lowered in concentration.

Karl's delight was ill concealed. As it became apparent that no one was going to volunteer, he smiled broadly. He glanced down the table and located Gus and Billy sitting quietly near the end. "How about you guys?" he taunted sarcastically. "Why aren't you volunteering your all for the good of the ranch?" Guffawing loudly, his mouth still half full of food, he turned back to Doug. "So, what are you gonna tell the committee? That the ranch has suddenly come down with cholera, and all our eager jousters are bedridden?"

Doug looked up from his plate. "We have a team of sorts."

"You and Tim! You call that a team? You've got to have four men."

"We do have a couple of others," Doug added. "I didn't get a chance to tell you because we got sidetracked talking about other things. Gus and Billy are also on the Circle Diamond team."

Karl's face flushed dark with anger. "Come off it! Those guys just refused to volunteer! I heard them myself!"

"My pitch was for extra guys," Doug answered

evenly. "Since they're already registered as team members with the committee, I guess they didn't figure I was talking to them."

Something that sounded like a chuckle came from the end of the table where Mr. Brookes was sitting, but when I glanced over he was busy wiping his lips with his napkin and it was impossible to tell what he was thinking.

I looked at Karl. It's a good thing the ranch dishes were made of sturdy china. The way he was attacking those pork chops with his knife and fork, I had an idea he was wishing one of them was Doug.

Mr. Brookes finished with his napkin. He put it in his lap and looked down the table to where Gus and Billy and Doug and I were sitting. His expression sobered. "I know you boys are doing this because you think the ranch should respond to the appeal from the rodeo committee, and I appreciate that. I'd hate to think that the Circle Diamond either wouldn't or couldn't try to help in a case like this. But as Karl says, jousting is a dangerous sport. You could be hurt, and I'm not prepared to sit back and let that happen. I suggest that the ranch send in its entry fee as tangible support for the event, but that you withdraw from actual competition."

"Come on, Dad! Everyone in the country would call us chicken!" Doug exclaimed. "Besides, it isn't just the entry fee that the committee is concerned about. It's also their reputation. They've billed this as a first-class tournament and they're planning to make it an annual event. Jousting experts from a lot of different centers have been invited. Unless there are enough entries to make it a real competition, the committee is going to look pretty foolish.''

Doug had been watching his father closely as he'd been talking. ''Besides,'' he added, the hint of a smile coming into his eyes, ''we want to do it.''

''Why? You've never shown the slightest interest in jousting before.''

''That's true, and we probably wouldn't have thought about it now — except for Tim, of course.'' He glanced at me. Without even a trace of guilt at the whopper he was telling, he added, ''Tim's been wanting to have a go at jousting ever since he heard about the Falkland rodeo. But Gus and Billy and I are strictly responding to the appeal from the rodeo committee. They need the big ranches to support them, and we don't want the Circle Diamond to let them down.''

He couldn't come right out and say it, of course, but I knew he was hoping his dad would understand that this was Gus's and Billy's way of proving they cared about the ranch.

It was obvious from Mr. Brookes's expression that he'd made the connection. The glimmer of a smile came into his eyes. ''Now that Karl has explained how dangerous jousting is and how he wouldn't want to do it, I think we should be glad we've got men like Gus and Billy who are willing to volunteer.''

I felt as if the sun had just been turned up to double brightness. Doug had been right! By registering for the jousting tournament, Gus and Billy had proved themselves! By the time the tournament was over everything would be just fine again. After all, how could any boss stay mad at two guys who really came up big for him? After Mr. Brookes saw them putting it on the line for the ranch's reputation, he'd forget all about a minor thing like the corral gate being left open, which meant there was no need for me to own up after all.

"However," Mr. Brookes's voice broke into my thoughts, "I still want whoever was responsible for leaving that corral gate open to be man enough to stand up and admit it. Otherwise, jousting team or no jousting team, Gus and Billy will continue to work under Karl's supervision."

Doug, Billy, Gus and Karl all said something in reply, but I couldn't hear over the sound of my world crashing.

I'd agreed to go into the jousting tournament so the guys could prove their loyalty. I'd thought that was enough. I was prepared to risk a few broken bones, but I wasn't prepared to slit my own throat by admitting that I'd been the one to leave the gate unfastened. What excuse could I give for not having owned up long ago? The other guys would never understand. As for Mr. Brookes, he'd already said what he thought of people who ran away. He'd probably send me packing, and how would that make my folks feel? There was no way I could say anything. Billy and Gus would just have to plead their own cases and hope for the best.

By this time most of the people had started to drift out of the dining room. Gus, Billy and Doug were halfway to the door. They must have been still talking about what Mr. Brookes had said because Doug's voice floated back to me.

"We can worry later about finding out who left that gate open. For the moment the important thing is doing a good job in the joust."

"Who's kidding who?" Billy replied, and his voice had that old hopeless ring. "Even if we pull off a win it's not going to change anything."

"It will if we find out who was really to blame," Doug insisted.

"As if anybody's gonna own up after all this time."

They disappeared through the doorway and I didn't hear any more.

I got up from the table. If Mr. Brookes was watching a ball game on TV I'd join him. At least that way I wouldn't have to do any more thinking.

I headed for the living room. Of all the rooms in the ranch house, I like it best. It's big and roomy and cheerful, with chintz-covered furniture, bright blue drapes and a rug so deep you sink into it as you walk. One whole wall is a huge window looking out over the countryside, while another is a huge fireplace. I could picture the blaze that would be roaring there on a winter evening.

Unfortunately the TV wasn't on. Mr. Brookes was sitting in his armchair talking to Mrs. Brookes and Hilary, who were on the sofa.

I started to leave again but Mr. Brookes saw me.

"Come in, Tim," he said. "We were just talking about you."

Reluctantly I moved through the doorway. I sat on a straight-backed leather-covered chair.

"I'm uneasy about your riding with the jousting team," Mr. Brookes said without any preamble.

"I think I should try to talk one of the other boys into riding in your place. They're not exactly eager, but I'm sure one of them will do it if I ask him."

He wasn't half as worried as I was, but what was Hilary going to think if I backed out now? I forced a smile. "It's okay. I'd like to try. Honest."

"Are you sure Doug hasn't talked you into it?"

"No," I replied. "I volunteered."

Hilary nodded. "He did, Dad. Doug told me, and I'm glad, because it solves all my problems."

Her dad looked at her in surprise, but his surprise was nothing compared with mine. Was she that eager to get rid of me?

"Sultan's still lame," she went on. "I've been working on his tendon for more than a week, but there's no way he'll be healthy by Saturday. I was preparing myself for a really boring rodeo, but now —" and she started to smile "— I can keep busy patching up the cuts and bruises on the Circle Diamond jousting team."

"Bring lots of splints and iodine, okay?" I told her.

Mrs. Brookes had been watching me with a funny soft look on her face. "Before you came your parents wrote and told us of the problems you were having in Winnipeg," she said quietly. "They were worried about you."

"Yes, I know."

"To be honest, I was worried, too. I wasn't sure how we'd all get along this summer." The soft look turned into a smile. "I'm going to write your mother and tell her that we couldn't possibly have had a nicer addition to our family."

I looked down at the rug because I was sure my guilt must show. I could feel myself shrivel. I couldn't have felt worse if she'd said I was a rotten houseguest. "I'm kind of tired," I mumbled, getting to my feet. "I think I'll catch some fresh air, then go to bed." Taking care not to look at anyone, I escaped outside into the safety of the darkness. The night air felt good against my cheeks and I started to relax. Then in the distance I heard a cow bawling for some calf that must have wandered far away. The cow sounded really worried, and that made me feel worse again.

"Tim! Wait!" Hilary called from the doorway. She ran to catch up. For a minute we walked in silence.

"Remember that conversation we had a couple of weeks ago?" Hilary said at last. I felt her hand creep into mine. "About how Doug seemed to feel responsible for Gus and Billy?"

"Uh-huh." It was hard to concentrate. The pressure of her fingers had started increasing ever so slightly for a moment, then relaxing, then increasing again. I couldn't decide whether or not to press back. I wanted to, but what if that scared her off and she let go? I settled on keeping a firm, even pressure and letting her do the variations.

"I got the impression then that you thought it was dumb for Doug to bother fighting their cause. But I was wrong. You're doing it, too."

"Just because I'm riding on the jousting team it doesn't mean —"

"You're not a horseman, Tim, and everybody knows it." She was looking straight at me.

"You're risking a lot of bruises and maybe even some broken bones so the ranch can have a team and so Billy and Gus can straighten things out with Dad." A tinge of extra color crept into her cheeks and her fingers went right on with their pressing. "That makes you pretty special in my book."

I tried to find the words to answer. Before I could, she added softly, "Thank you for getting involved."

Now I felt worse than ever! "Hilary," I blurted, "where's the dividing line? How far do you go?"

She looked confused.

"When it comes to sticking your neck out for somebody, when do you say, sorry, I can't do any more because it will work against me?"

She looked at me thoughtfully. "I don't think that could ever happen."

"Sure it could."

She shook her head. "If you take up somebody's cause it's because you believe in it. Even though working for it might cost you something — even a lot sometimes — it'd never work against you."

"Then let's put it this way. If, in order to keep on helping somebody, you had to do something that would bring trouble on yourself, should you do it?"

"Would you ever feel right if you didn't?"

"What if there was too much at stake?"

She was silent for a minute. "I guess you've got to decide a question like that on the basis of relative losses," she said at last.

"Who stands to lose the most?"

"Uh-huh. And who's best able to recover and start again."

I was so deep in thought after that remark that I scarcely felt her fingers slip from mine. It wasn't till I found myself standing all alone in the darkness that I realized she'd gone.

Twelve

*I*t was Thursday again. Not a nothing Thursday, as so many Thursdays seem to be, but a problem one. For the first time I was beginning to understand what John Donne had meant when he said no man is an island.

We studied Donne in school last year. Whenever we're studying a special author Mrs. Beckstein assigns a lot of different things that author has written, tells us to read them, then picks half a dozen different quotes that she says are really well known and asks us to explain what they mean.

As a rule I do at least some of the reading, but the night we were supposed to be studying Donne was the night Brad had picked for the final blue-ribbon-special drag race. It was a question of priorities, and Donne lost. As a result, next morning, when Mrs. Beckstein started tossing off quotes I wasn't exactly well prepared. I was okay on some — I could at least make a stab at them — but others were tough.

"No man is an island" fell into the tough category, and that was the one Mrs. Beckstein called on me to explain.

I swallowed, took a deep breath and got to my feet.

That was the first rule for getting through secondary-school English, I'd discovered — be polite and get to your feet when you have to answer a question. The second was never to come right out and say what you thought an author meant, even if you figured you knew. Chances were almost ninety-nine to one you'd be wrong. The smart thing was to make it sound as if you were really impressed by the passage, only unable to find the right words to explain how you were feeling.

That's what I did on the "No man is an island" question. Then I sat back and waited for Mrs. Beckstein to stick somebody else with the chance to say something intelligent.

The somebody else was Brad.

If it's a mistake for me to try to analyze literature, it's a disaster for Brad to do it. It's not that he hasn't any imagination — he has, lots of it. Only it seems to be all channeled in one direction. Besides, when he had made up his list of priorities the previous night, he put drag racing ahead of English homework, too.

For a second after Mrs. Beckstein called on him he sat in silence, his face wearing a puzzled frown. I crossed my fingers and sent wordless messages across the rows of desks, urging him to go on keeping quiet, because I knew from experience what could happen if he let his sense of humor get the better of him. Either the messages didn't get through or he ignored them, because the next thing I knew the puzzled frown had gone and that all too familiar gleam had appeared deep in his eyes.

"Drag racing," he answered innocently. "I think that's what this Donne guy is talking about, and he must have done a lot of it, because he's right."

Mrs. Beckstein looked completely confused.

"Work it out," Brad went on, sounding more pleased with himself with every word. "Let's say you're cruising down Ellice Avenue, or maybe Notre Dame, doing a hundred and ten kilometers, and some dumb pedestrian steps off the safety island right into your path. You've gotta choose — the concrete or the pedestrian. Donne is absolutely right. Who's gonna deliberately wreck his car just to —"

The rest of his words were buried under a roar of laughter from the class.

Mrs. Beckstein was livid. She sent Brad to the principal's office and gave the whole class a detention. It was for an hour, and for the whole sixty minutes Mrs. Beckstein explained in detail that the parallel hadn't been safety islands and pedestrians, but islands and continents. She made us all copy off the board, "No man is an island . . . every man is a piece of the continent."

I didn't know what that meant, either, but it didn't matter because Wordsworth replaced Donne the following week in English and I didn't have to think about "No man is an island" again.

But the past couple of days I hadn't been able to stop thinking about it, I guess because I finally understood what Donne meant. We weren't islands, we were parts of a continent, and my shoreline was hooked right on to Gus's and Billy's.

Darn it all, why wasn't every man an island? It would have made everything so much simpler.

At least there's one advantage to having problems — you haven't time to worry about anything else. I went through the practice jousting sessions that Thursday like a hardened stunt rider. Time after time on Doug's signal I galloped down the tilt with lance at the ready, met Gus or Billy racing toward me from the opposite direction and went flying.

"You know what?" Doug told me after about my tenth fall. He was looking down at me from the lordly height of his horse's back as I lay in the sawdust we'd piled up in the center of the track. "You fall like a real pro. You don't even look scared. I told you we'd make a jouster out of you by Saturday."

"And even that old bay mare seems to have learned to respect you," Gus put in. "She's given up fighting and comes along the tilt like a well-trained charger."

It was true. For some strange reason Brownie had stopped pushing me around and was letting me make the decisions. It was a good feeling to know I commanded respect from somebody — even if only from a horse.

I scrambled to my feet and brushed off the sawdust. "Do you think we should try the grand melee?" I asked.

"You mean a half grand melee," Doug said. "We need two full teams for the real thing."

"Okay, a half grand melee. Should we practice it?"

Doug turned to Gus and Billy. "What d'you think?"

They nodded agreement.

"Okay," Doug said. "But everybody remember to hang onto your opponent if you feel him coming out of the saddle, and ease him down gently. We can't afford to have any casualties. We're not exactly overburdened with guys wanting to ride as substitutes."

The grand melee wasn't as bad as I'd expected. In fact, being wrestled off your horse with a little weight-bearing assistance wasn't nearly as painful or nerve-racking as being jarred off by somebody's lance in the regular joust.

Mr. Brookes had said we could forget about the ranch work till after the tournament, so we practiced most of the day with just a few intermissions for applying liniment to our bruises. By mid-afternoon we had attracted a crowd of interested spectators, including Hilary and Mrs. Brookes. We conscripted Hilary to serve as our practice wench, but it was probably just as well that she wasn't going to be the wench in the real tournament. It's not easy to keep your mind on the race when someone like Hilary is sitting in your lap.

The only one who didn't come around was Karl. I guess he was too busy.

At dinner that evening the wisecracking department was working overtime. "Are the condemned men enjoying their last meal?" someone asked.

"Enjoy that steak. Next time it's on the menu you guys may not have any teeth."

"Do you like liquids? I understand that's all the hospital gives you while you're in traction waiting for bones to heal."

It wasn't just the ranch hands who were doing the teasing — Mr. Brookes was, too. He was laughing and joking with all four of us, Gus and Billy included, without the slightest trace of any coldness or disapproval.

All at once I realized I'd been dumb to get myself all worked up about islands and continents. Mr. Brookes wasn't mad at Gus and Billy any longer. Now I could forget about everything except living through this tournament.

Actually, I realized, by riding on the jousting team I was doing a far bigger favor for Gus and Billy than I'd ever have done by owning up. By agreeing to be the fourth rider, I was giving them a chance to square things with Mr. Brookes and Karl, and at the same time to show everybody in the area what good stuff they were made of. By owning up, on the other hand, I would have ruined everything. They wouldn't have been able to do any impressing or show anybody anything, because a jousting team had to have four riders and theirs would have had only three. I'd have been sent packing.

One day last winter in Winnipeg a bunch of us were roughhousing in the school washroom, and somehow the sink got knocked down. Another day so many of us were crowded in Brad's truck that he couldn't see very well, and when he backed up to get out of the parking lot he crunched the fender of the car parked behind. Both times a couple of the guys thought we should say something — tell the principal about the sink, maybe, and leave a note on the car, but Rory talked them out of it. It wasn't going to make any difference, he pointed out. The guy's insurance would pay to fix his fender, and the school's janitors would fix the sink, so what difference did it make whether or not we got into it? "Let sleeping dogs lie" was the expression he used.

It had been good advice then, and it was good advice now. The jousting tournament would take its course, and by the time it was over there'd be nothing to worry about. Gus and Billy would be heroes, Mr. Brookes and Karl would be happy because the ranch would have come up big, I wouldn't be in anybody's bad books and everything would be back to normal.

With that decided, after dinner I went in search of Hilary.

Thirteen

I found her down by the barn putting hot foments on Sultan's strained tendon.

"Any chance he'll be ready in time for the rodeo?" I asked, watching her.

She shook her head. "But that's okay. There'll be lots of other chances to do barrels before the summer is over, and there's no way I'm going to risk racing him if he isn't absolutely a hundred percent. Barrels are about the hardest thing you can put a horse through, and if he isn't sound to start with he's sure to end up getting hurt."

She unwrapped the piece of flannel she was holding around the swollen ankle joint, dipped it in warm ointment, wrung it out and rewrapped Sultan's leg.

For a moment she worked in silence. Then, still concentrating on what she was doing, she said softly. "You've worked out that problem, haven't you?"

I jumped. Was mind reading another of her talents?

"You pretended the other evening that if helping somebody else was too expensive you'd hold back, but I knew you didn't mean it."

I started breathing again. For a second I'd forgotten about that conversation.

Hilary soaked the flannel once again, only this time after she wrapped it around Sultan's leg she added several firm twists of vet wrap to hold it in place. "I knew you'd help Gus and Billy square things."

She straightened up. She was looking straight at me. Her eyes were soft and warm and her lips were slightly parted. Before I realized what she was planning, she moved so close I could feel her breath on my cheek. Then she raised her chin and gazed right into my face.

I felt a wave of panic. In a desperate attempt to cover my confusion I took a step backward and nodded at the horse behind her. "D'you figure he'll be okay now?" I rattled quickly. "If it's okay to leave him, d'you want to go for a walk or something?"

Her chin lowered and she laughed. But it wasn't the hard, brittle laugh of a week ago. It was a warm, friendly, amused laugh, as if I'd just said something really funny.

She must be nervous, I decided. That must be why she laughed, because what was funny about somebody asking if she wanted to go for a walk? "Do you?" I asked again.

She was still smiling. "Uh-huh." She drew the word out so it was almost singing. "I'd like to, only I can't go tonight. I promised Doug I'd help him get the jousting costumes ready. Let's make it next week, as soon as the rodeo's over, okay?"

She continued to watch me with that warm, smiling look and I felt myself go all tingly inside. Before I could get my act together to answer, she was gone.

Fourteen

*I*t wasn't only Hilary who had to help Doug get the jousting stuff ready. The following day, Gus and Billy and I had to help, too.

When Hilary had referred to our uniforms as costumes I'd felt a bit insulted. They were armor for mounted combat, and she ought to have called them that.

She probably would have, except for one small detail — they were made of cardboard.

Not everything. The lances were made of bamboo and the helmets were made of plastic, but the shields and breastplates were cardboard. It was thick, sturdy cardboard, but it *was* cardboard, and I had an awkward feeling that on Saturday and Sunday when an opposing knight came charging toward me on a galloping horse, his lance at the ready, such a shield wasn't going to offer quite the sense of security I was hoping for.

The one consolation was that the bamboo lances weren't sharp: instead of having pointed ends they had flat ones. But just the same . . .

First thing on Friday we assembled and adjusted our costumes. It was the adjusting that took the time. When the eye slit on a helmet is two inches too low, the wearer is at a distinct disadvantage. So is he when his chest armor is so big it tucks up under his chin. But at last we got things organized. Then once again we rehearsed all the events. After that we groomed and polished the horses so they'd look nice in the rodeo parade. By the time we were finished it was bedtime.

I might as well have stayed up, for all the sleep I got. All I could think of as I tossed and turned and tried to relax was what was going to happen tomorrow. Mathematics has never been my best subject, but even I could figure out that if a galloping horse travels at about thirty miles an hour, riders on two galloping horses meeting head on were going to meet with quite an impact.

By six o'clock on Saturday morning we were down at the barn collecting our gear for loading.

At seven Hilary appeared in the doorway.

Doug let the tack he was holding fall noisily to the wooden floor as he made a show of looking at his watch. "Socializing at seven in the morning? My dear sister, what on earth can be the attraction?" He grinned pointedly in my direction.

I had the stupidity to blush.

Hilary wasn't a bit embarrassed. "I came to wish you good luck." She reached up and gave him a sisterly kiss on the cheek. Doug smiled and hugged her.

She shook hands with Gus and Billy.

It was my turn. When she turned to me, her eyes were soft and laughing.

Ever since last night I'd been kicking myself for being such a dolt. Why hadn't I kissed her when she'd obviously been inviting me to? Well, this time I was ready. This time, even though it would be kind of embarrassing with the other guys looking on, as soon as she moved up close to me and lifted her chin, I'd . . .

"Good luck, Tim, and be careful. Okay?" She'd stopped walking when she was still a whole foot and a half away and she was holding out her hand.

I felt as if the winning ticket on Lotto 649 had just blown out of my hand and disappeared.

But the next second I forgot all about Lotto 649, for the expression in her eyes wasn't just teasing — it was warm, and soft and caring as well. And her fingers as they closed over mine started squeezing in that special on-off way of hers.

I tried to say something but I was too flustered to think clearly, and before I could recover she released my hand and was on her way out of the barn.

It was ten minutes before I could get my mind on what I was doing, and an hour before Doug stopped smiling every time he caught my eye.

At nine o'clock we were ready to leave the ranch.

It's a fair drive from the Circle Diamond to Falkland — a hundred kilometers east to Kamloops, then another hundred south. It took close to two and a half hours.

When we got there the place looked like Hollywood North. There were flags flying, recorded trumpet music blaring out of a dozen loudspeakers, costumed dancing girls rehearsing and mounted contestants practicing fast starts and quick turns. Already the spectators' stands were starting to fill.

In front of the stands the wooden tilt had been erected, with small flags and standards mounted at intervals along its length. Halfway along, at the point where the opposing jousters would meet head on, two men were busy unloading a truck-load of sawdust and raking it into a nice cushiony mattress.

"Let's get the bad news over with," Doug said, coming up to where Gus and Billy and I were standing beside the horse van. He had a printed program in his hand. "Let's see what we're committed to."

We all peered at the sheet.

The first item on the program was the grand parade, scheduled for noon.

"There's a parade to start things off each day," Doug explained. "We all march in to a fanfare of trumpets — first the court dancing maidens, then the rodeo contestants, then the teams of knights accompanied by their squires."

Four sons of the men on the ranch had been recruited to serve as squires, one for each of us.

It was their responsibility to help the jousters mount, to hand them their lances and shields, to hold their horses at the head of the tilt until the jousting master gave the signal for combat to begin, to retrieve any dropped weapons and to catch our horses should we be unseated. They were probably also supposed to wipe the blood off

the nice clean grass should that be necessary, but
no one felt like mentioning that.

"There are four events scheduled for today,"
Doug went on, studying the printed sheet. "First
is the half-lance relay."

I felt like cheering. There was nothing particularly difficult or dangerous about the half-
lance relay. I might even manage to come out of
it with some self-respect.

"Next is the wench rescue race," Doug continued, "then pig sticking and finally ringing."

"That's it for today?" I asked with relief.

"That's it for today, Sir Timothy. That doesn't
sound too terrible, does it?"

"It sounds terrific. We might even be healthy
enough when we finish to head over to the stock
barns and catch some of the rodeo events. I'd like
to see how the other guys from the ranch make
out."

"No one from the ranch is entered in anything," Doug said.

"You mean they've all dropped out?" I knew
Hilary had dropped out of the barrels because of
Sultan's strained tendon, but I'd expected that all
the cowboys would be competing in something.

"No one wants to miss a moment of our live
action," Doug replied. His voice was dry. "And
I don't know that I blame them. Particularly not
on Sunday and Monday."

I felt my stomach take a fourteen-story plunge.
"What's on Sunday and Monday?"

Doug pointed at the program. Under Sunday
was just one big heading: jousting. Twelve individual two-man contests were listed. The

members of the Flying M team would compete against the men from the Double J, and the four men from the T Bar T ranch were up against our team from the Circle Diamond. The two teams that scored highest in these initial contests would square off in four final events to determine the winning team.

"We're lucky to meet the T Bar T in the first round, instead of the other teams," Doug said, still studying the list. "T Bar T is probably the easiest to beat."

"How would they have decided who would meet who?" Gus asked.

"Luck of the draw, probably," Doug told him. "But we sure won't complain."

As far as I was concerned, it wasn't going to make any difference which team we met first, and I was doing a quick mental calculation of how many falls I'd have to take before the tournament was over when Gus said, "What about Monday?"

"If we're still alive by then, Monday shouldn't be quite as bad. They probably want to keep the jousting short on the last afternoon so everyone can catch the finals in the rodeo, because all that's listed for us is the grand melee."

"At least there's no dagger swoop," I said.

Doug smiled, then looked at his watch. "It's already after eleven. If we're going to be dressed and ready for the grand parade in less than an hour, we'd better get these horses unloaded and get organized."

There was no time for any more talk or even for any regrets. We were too busy. In fact we'd only finished dolling up our horses in their scarlet and blue skirts and struggling into our own costumes when the recorded trumpet music signaled the beginning of the grand parade.

I felt foolish riding in formation with Doug, Gus and Billy, escorted by four grinning twelve-year-old squires, with everybody dressed up as if we were going to a Halloween party, but the spectators enjoyed it. They were clapping and cheering and having a great time.

"Come on, Circle Diamond!" The cheer floated over the sound of the music as we passed in front of the stands.

Doug waved his lance toward the shouter and bowed in his saddle.

I wondered if it was Hilary. I knew she was sitting up there somewhere. A warm, cozy feeling started up deep in my stomach — different from anything I'd ever felt before. It was really something to be part of a team.

The feeling stayed with me all day. Every time one of us did something right we could hear the sounds of encouragement from the stands. Every time we took a beating there were groans of sympathy. Boy, what a difference those spectators make when you're out there competing.

The half-lance relay went just about according to plan. Gus rode first and when he'd completed the four-hundred-meter sprint around the tilt and back again he was about half a length ahead of the Double J rider, and four or five lengths ahead of the other two.

Billy was already in motion as Gus swept past him. He grabbed the lance and was off at a gallop before the Double J rider had a firm grip on his lance. That split second meant another two lengths added to our lead by the time Billy had completed his circle and swung around to me.

I wanted to get a fast start, too. I grabbed the lance, managed to hang on to it without dropping it, which was something I'd been having nightmares about, then booted Brownie.

Maybe fast starts are something you have to live with for longer than three days. That boot must have been a let's-head-off-for-a-nice-little-ride boot, instead of a run-for-your-life one. Brownie set off at a polite canter, shaking her mane as if she was thoroughly enjoying herself. By the time I had convinced her with my heels and my voice that we were really in a hurry, the Double J rider had left us behind.

As I rounded the tilt and headed back for the start of the relay line all I could see was Doug's outstretched hand. As Brownie and I galloped the final twenty meters, Doug was already moving.

"Okay!" he shouted as we came abreast of him. The lance was wrenched out of my fingers as Doug's horse dug in his hind legs and shot forward at a gallop.

We had made no mistake in putting Doug last. That horse of his was reputed to be the fastest quarter horse on the ranch, and he proved it right then. At the halfway mark Doug was on the Double J rider's heels. At the turn Doug cut him off and raced for home.

Good old Circle Diamond had taken a lead with five points for a win. Gus and Billy were thumping me on the back, telling me what a good job I'd done, and Doug was grinning from ear to ear.

Then it was the wench rescue race.

The thing I'd been worrying about in this one was that I'd get the route wrong around the barrels. In spite of Doug's lessons and his maps and my going over the whole thing time after time in my mind, I was afraid when the race started I'd be too excited to remember.

But it wasn't a problem at all. The three barrels were placed so far apart and the path we were to ride was so clearly gouged in the soft dirt by the hoofprints of the other horses there was no way I could make a mistake. Also, old Brownie must have done barrels before. Even if I hadn't known how to make the circles, she did.

She even stood still for me to dismount, untie the wench and struggle back on board again, pulling the long-skirted maiden with me. Most of the other horses didn't. They spun around, rearing and bucking and making things as tough as they could for the poor riders.

If Brownie'd done that I'd still be out there.

Gus and Billy didn't manage as well in the wench rescue as they'd done in the relay. Doug was the only person on our team who really did well. As a result we came in second. The Double J beat us.

The pig-sticking honors went to the Flying M. They had two knights who didn't miss a single peg. Everybody else missed at least a couple, and I missed all but a couple. The only way I got those two was by riding so slowly that I lost points for overtime. All in all it wasn't exactly a triumph, but at least we came third.

Which was one spot higher than we did in the ringing.

Obviously, the other teams had been practicing — either that or they had better distance vision and steadier hands. The T Bar T came out on top there.

At the end of the first day it was still pretty even: there were only about six points separating all four teams.

I was feeling about twelve feet high when we went in to dinner that night.

The competitors were staying in different motels in Falkland, so the rodeo committee had decided to have everybody eat together. They had set up one central dining room with separate tables for the competitors from each ranch. That night Doug, Gus, Billy and I were sitting on one side of the Circle Diamond table with Hilary sitting next to me, and every time I looked at her she smiled.

One by one the other ranch hands came in and joined us, and everyone had something to say about what a great job we were doing, and how they'd be out there cheering for us tomorrow. Mr. Brookes said the same. Just like last night, he congratulated all four of us and seemed really pleased.

I bet Karl would have congratulated us, too, if he'd been there, but he didn't come in for dinner.

Fifteen

Karl didn't come in for breakfast the next morning, either.

Nobody paid much notice except maybe Mr. Brookes. Everybody else figured Karl was busy attending to ranch business, and they were too interested in quizzing us about our jousting tactics to give him a second thought. Today was the big day as far as the Circle Diamond jousting team was concerned. Before the day was over everyone at the tournament would know whether or not we deserved to call ourselves jousters.

As we'd already discovered, our first four jousts were to be against the four knights of the T Bar T team, while the Double J would fight the Flying M. The two teams piling up the most points would then advance to round two and fight four more individual contests against each other.

I couldn't decide whether to hope that we did well for the sake of the ranch, or that we didn't, so I wouldn't have to joust twice.

"I still say we're lucky to have drawn the T Bar T," Doug remarked as we were getting ready.

"There's no reason we can't beat them and move into the second round."

I could think of a reason — a good one — but I didn't want to tell him.

"I'll go first," Doug went on. "Billy will be second, then Gus and finally Tim."

"Why are you putting Tim last?" Billy asked.

"Because that way he'll know just how much he has to put out. There's no point in his taking a chance on being hurt if we've already lost it on points. In that case he might as well take an easy fall as soon as he's hit. But if we're ahead, then he'll know he has to do his darnedest to stay in the saddle."

"Can we do the same?" Gus asked with a grin. "Take a dive if it looks like we've lost?"

"No way. You've got to go all out for the ranch no matter what. I've an idea Karl will be much more willing to forgive and forget if you're bruised and bleeding and wrapped in bandages."

"He's probably expecting nothing less than our lives," Gus said dryly. His lips were smiling, but his eyes were serious.

By the time the slave maidens had finished their dance and the trumpet music heralded the start of the jousting bouts, we were all pretty tense.

Doug's squire handed him his shield and lance.

"Good luck, Doug," I called.

He smiled. Then, with his squire in attendance, he moved toward the end of the tilt to wait for the signal to charge.

It was a good thing we'd been given squires. Even with the boy holding the horse's head, it was all Doug could do to keep the animal in position. With the blaring music, the flags flapping in the wind and all the people yelling, the poor horse was almost as scared as I was.

The trumpet sounded.

Doug flew down that tilt like a cavalry officer in the Charge of the Light Brigade. The T Bar T rider was coming a little slower, or he seemed to be.

When they met, Doug made a powerful lunge, but at the last second the other guy's horse edged sideways just far enough for Doug's lance to miss. He didn't move far enough away from the tilt to be disqualified, just far enough to edge past, which meant they had to do it all over again.

They would be given three tries. If at the end of three they had still failed to strike each other, it would be ruled a draw with no points scored either way.

They went back to their places, one knight at each end of the tilt, and charged again.

This time Doug didn't miss. He caught the other guy squarely in the center of his shield, and the T Bar T rider went sprawling in the sawdust, shield and lance flying.

It was Billy's turn.

Billy didn't unseat his opponent, but on three straight passes he struck his opponent's shield, so he got points for that.

So far we were doing fine.

As Gus came down the tilt on his first run, the T Bar T rider caught his shield. It looked for a moment as if Gus was going flying, but he managed to keep his seat. On the second pass he was ready. He galloped faster this time to give himself the weight advantage, then timed his lunge perfectly. He caught the other rider's shield dead center. The T Bar T knight flew backward out of the saddle and the next second was lying in that nice cushion of sawdust.

Then it was me.

I was so scared my knees were shaking. I could hardly hold my lance. Good old Brownie knew it. It was just like that first time when we were practicing. We started down the tilt and as soon as my opponent hove into view, lance outstretched, Brownie headed for the hills.

I collected her and went back to my end of the tilt and waited for the second pass to be signaled.

The same thing happened.

This time the crowd laughed.

I remember thinking to myself as I rode to the end of the tilt for my third pass that it was the last one. I just had to do it once more and I'd be finished with the jousting.

Then I felt Doug's hand on Brownie's rein. I hadn't expected him to be there — it should have been my squire waiting to attend me.

"Stop shaking and concentrate," he said, his voice firm. "If you let Brownie pull out of the circle again you'll be disqualified, and so will the team. Hold her in to the tilt. It doesn't matter if you get knocked off, or if the other guy gets a strike on your shield. We've got enough points to stay in this thing, just so long as you don't get us disqualified."

I met his eyes. His expression wasn't excited and happy any more. It was worried. In fact it was almost resigned. He didn't think I could do it.

Right then and there I smartened up. If I got thrown it wouldn't be the end of the world, I told myself.

When the trumpet sounded the charge, I jabbed old Brownie in the flanks as she'd never been jabbed before. "Now smarten up!" I told her sternly. "Do what I tell you!"

To my amazement, she did. Straight down the tilt she galloped, directly into the lance the T Bar T rider was holding out for me.

All I remember as I left the saddle was yelling, as Doug had told me to do, and tossing my lance and shield clear so I wouldn't fall on them. Then I was in the sawdust. It didn't hurt at all.

Doug was the first to help me up. "Way to go, Sir Timothy! That was terrific!" He was beaming.

I struggled to my feet. There didn't seem to be any bones broken.

Gus and Billy were waiting on the sidelines, grinning from ear to ear.

Then it was the Double J's turn to joust against the Flying M. The first Double J rider managed to unseat his opponent, but exactly the opposite thing happened with the number-two riders. Then the third knights from each team confronted each other.

"These two aren't as good as the first pair," Gus remarked as we were watching from the sidelines.

They weren't. Three successive passes saw neither knight succeed in striking his opponent's shield, with the result that no points were scored.

The fourth contest went to the Double J contestant, which meant we would meet the four Double J riders in the second round of jousts.

I felt my heart sink. Any more tumbles into that sawdust from a gallop really didn't appeal to me. But there was no retreating now.

For the second round we kept the same order. This time both Gus and Doug threw their opponents, Billy's contest was a draw and I hit the sawdust as usual.

After supper that night the official results were posted. Everyone flocked over to see exactly how things stood.

Standing to read those results was like being middle row in the sardine can, but it was worth it to read Circle Diamond up there at the top.

"Well done, boys," Mr. Brookes said, moving over beside us. "I'm proud of you."

Doug gave his Stetson a casual tip, trying to seem unconcerned, but I knew him well enough by then to know how pleased he was. His dad's approval meant a lot to him.

"I hate to drag you away, Doug," Mr. Brookes went on, "but there are a couple of breeders here I'd like you to meet. Someday you'll be running the ranch, and it's always nice to put a face to a signature." He led the way out of the crowd with Doug beside him.

"Wanna go for a Coke?" Billy asked, turning to Gus and me.

We moved to join him.

But as I was pushing and shoving to make a path for myself out of the crush, somebody's foot caught my spur and pulled it loose. Quickly I bent to retrieve it. If somebody stepped on it and bent the rowel, it'd be no good for tomorrow.

It was like being a midget in a forest of redwoods. All I could see was legs and feet standing in rows all around me. Where the heck was that spur? Somebody must have kicked it.

I continued to bend double, studying the floor.

Darn it all, how was I going to get old Brownie to put a little effort into her performance if I didn't find it?

"You'll let me know, then, by noon tomorrow?" a voice sounded over my head.

I forgot about the spur and started trying to fight back to a standing position, because the voice was Karl's. I wanted to hear what he had to say about those terrific results. I was sure he'd be pleased.

"I haven't had a chance to discuss this with Brookes yet," Karl's voice rasped over my head, "but I'm sure he'll be in agreement. We both feel that in an operation as big as ours it's essential to have dependable men, and unfortunately a couple of ours just haven't measured up."

I forgot about trying to straighten up and ducked lower. It was as if the air had suddenly gone thin, and I couldn't breathe properly. A pulse started pounding in my head.

"I'll be letting them go before the end of the week," Karl's voice continued. "If you're interested, let me know by noon tomorrow, otherwise I'll sign on a couple of fellows from the T Bar T. We're too busy this time of year to try to run a ranch shorthanded."

The crowd pushed me away and I couldn't hear any more.

There was my spur. It had been kicked against the wall. No one had stepped on it, but somehow that didn't seem to matter any longer.

Sixteen

I hardly remember fighting my way out of the crowd. Gus and Billy weren't that far ahead of me, only about fifty paces. They were headed for the concession stand, and I knew they were walking slowly to give me a chance to catch up, but I turned the other way. If I went anywhere near them they'd be sure to guess something was wrong from the look on my face. I had to think.

I headed away from the traffic toward the cattle barns. One of the box stalls was empty. It had a couple of nice big hay bales piled in one corner, so I sprawled on top of them.

Square one, that's where I was, right back at square one, only with everything a hundred times worse than it had been the first time around.

Darn it all, why couldn't Donne have been wrong?

I checked the time. Doug was sure to be finished talking business with those breeders by this time, I decided.

I found him sitting on the grass outside the dining hall, talking to Gus and Billy.

"Hey! Here's Sir Timothy!" he greeted me as I walked up. "Why the face of doom? Tomorrow can't be all that much worse than today, and we lived through that."

I knew if I stopped to think I'd never manage to say anything, so in a rush of words I told him what I'd overheard Karl saying, then tacked on without even a comma, "It was me in the barn that day when Gambler got loose. You've got to tell your dad right away before Karl has a chance to sign on those two new hands."

I was out of breath and shaking but I'd said it. The smile went out of Doug's eyes. "Run that by me again?"

"I went into the barn for a sleep, only I slept too long, and when I raced out of there I didn't take the time to close the gate properly. You've got to tell your dad before —"

"Why didn't you own up sooner?" Doug demanded. There was a firm, authoritative expression on his face that I'd never seen there before.

I glanced from his face to Gus's and Billy's. I could read hurt and disbelief in their eyes. Fighting down my embarrassment, I managed, "At first I didn't think it mattered — not when you guys found Gambler right away and he was okay. Then I didn't want to say anything because I was scared everybody'd be mad at me and I'd be sent home."

Surprise replaced the cold anger on Doug's face. "But I got the feeling that was the one thing you wanted above everything else."

"It was, at first, but then I got to like it here. I changed my mind. I wanted to stay."

Then I glanced at Gus and Billy. They looked like two friendly puppies who'd just been kicked by someone they thought was their friend. They probably wouldn't even want me to ride on the jousting team with them any longer, and I didn't blame them. I would feel exactly the same if some clod had left me to take the blame for something he had done.

"Maybe this whole thing is going to work out okay after all." Doug's quiet voice broke into my confusion. He was no longer talking to me, he was talking to Gus and Billy. "If Tim had spoken up right away it would have saved you guys a couple of uncomfortable weeks, but it wouldn't have changed things in the long run. Karl would still have gone on looking for things to complain about and ways to try to fire you. Now maybe Dad will see how you two get blamed for things even when Karl hasn't any proof."

A gleam of interest came into Gus's and Billy's faces.

"Also," Doug went on, "this tournament is giving everybody in the district the chance to see you do your stuff. If Karl does keep climbing your backs, you won't have to worry any more about being able to find another job. Any one of the other ranches will hire you."

The gleams turned into smiles.

But the mention of Karl had reminded me. "You've got to tell your dad," I urged for the third time. "Right away. Once Karl has signed on those new men it could be too late. He could say that —"

The words dried up, for Doug was shaking his head.

"Aren't you going to tell him?" I asked.

"Nope. You are, Sir Timothy. Having come this far, you can't crawl back now."

A yawning cavern opened up inside. It had been bad enough telling Doug and Gus and Billy. How was I ever going to tell Mr. Brookes?

"You can't tell him tonight, though," Doug went on, "because he's spending the evening with a couple of those breeders he introduced me to. But that shouldn't be a problem. If you can't talk to him, neither can Karl. As long as you speak to him before Karl does in the morning, everything should be okay."

I wasn't sure I agreed. What if Karl didn't bother to check with Mr. Brookes? What if he was so sure Mr. Brookes would follow his advice that he decided to go ahead and hire those two new hands without checking at all? I'd seen enough of Karl in the month I'd been at the Circle Diamond to know that the most important thing in his life was self-image. Once he'd committed himself to hiring new hands he wasn't going to back down.

Sure he'd tell Mr. Brookes how sorry he was about having fired Gus and Billy before he'd found out the truth about the Gambler incident. He'd say how much he wished he could undo things, only he'd add that now two new hands had been hired he couldn't go back on the deal without making the ranch look stupid. Then he'd drop the hint that the whole thing was my fault for having been so chicken about owning up, and Mr. Brookes would agree with him.

I sure wished somebody could tell Mr. Brookes tonight. However, since that wasn't possible, I might as well go to bed. In fact, I'd better go to bed. With the team jousting schedule for tomorrow I needed all the sleep I could get.

Seventeen

I might as well have stayed up. Last Friday night had been nothing compared with this.

At last, to my relief, it was daylight and I could stop trying to get to sleep. I showered and had breakfast. Then I went in search of Mr. Brookes.

But everything seemed to be working against me. A meeting of the Cattlemen's Association had been scheduled for all morning in the dining room, and Mr. Brookes was on the executive.

"What am I gonna do?" I asked Doug frantically.

"Wait outside the door," he replied calmly. "The meeting can't go on forever, because sooner or later they're going to need to get this room ready for lunch. Catch Dad as soon as he comes out."

I took up a position in the grass directly outside.

I felt as if I'd put down roots, and still no one had emerged from the meeting.

Actually, there wasn't all that much activity around at all. A couple of hands wandered by en route to the cattle barns, but that was about all. I guess most of the people were taking it easy and resting up for the events scheduled to start at noon.

Then about eleven o'clock I saw Karl. He was emerging from the judges' tent. As he sauntered across the yard there was a smug, self-satisfied grin on his face.

My heart sank. Did that mean he'd finalized the deal with the new hands? But surely he wouldn't have been doing that in the judges' tent.

Before I had a chance to wonder any more, the door behind me opened. With a rush of chatter, the people from the cattlemen's meeting erupted into the fresh air.

At last! There was Mr. Brookes.

Gathering my courage I moved up beside him.

I didn't even stop to rehearse what I wanted to say. I just blurted, "It was me in the barn a couple of weeks ago, sir, not Billy and Gus." I explained what had happened, then went on to tell him about the conversation I'd overheard between Karl and the ranch hands.

Mr. Brookes listened with a serious, thoughtful expression on his face. When the flood of words subsided, he asked me the same questions that Doug had and I gave him the same answers.

"Only it's not fair for Karl to fire Gus and Billy for something I did," I ended. "Will you explain to him and make sure he understands?"

My dad is always after me to look people in the eye when I talk to them. The reason you should do it, he says, is because it shows the other person that you're being honest and straightforward and aren't afraid to take responsibility for what you've done. But I discovered right then that there's another reason. Looking somebody in the eye gives you a chance to see that person's changing expression.

I'd expected that Mr. Brookes would look pretty disgusted with me for having waited this long to own up about what had happened, and that he'd be pretty mad. But to my amazement there was understanding and even a hint of sympathy in his eyes as he gazed at me.

"I'm glad you've told me, Tim," he said quietly. "I'll speak to Karl. But I'd also like to speak to Gus and Billy. Ask them to come and see me, will you, as soon as the jousting tournament is over?"

The jousting tournament! It was almost eleven-thirty, and I had to be dressed and ready for the parade at twelve. "Yes, sir!" I told him as I tore out of there.

Halfway back to the barn I stopped. Karl had told those new hands he wanted an answer by twelve at the latest. It was almost half-past eleven. What if they'd already spoken to him and he'd signed their contracts? What if it was already too late?

"Tim! Hurry up!" Doug's voice cut across the dry dirt yard toward me.

I started running again. Maybe it was too late and maybe it wasn't, but I couldn't worry about it now. Item number one at this point was finishing the jousting tournament.

Eighteen

"**D**id you tell him? What did he say?" Doug asked as I came panting up to where the others were putting the finishing touches on their costumes.

I repeated exactly what had happened.

Doug nodded thoughtfully.

"Is he really gonna speak to Karl about us?" Gus asked.

"He promised he would." I didn't think there was any point in adding that I just hoped he'd be in time. "He wants to speak to you and Billy as well. He asked me to tell you to come and see him as soon as the jousting events are over."

"What about?" Gus sounded worried.

"He didn't say."

At that moment the loudspeaker system burst into life. "Ladies and gentlemen, your attention please," the metallic voice shouted. "It has been suggested by a senior representative of the leading team in this tournament, the Circle Diamond, that the initial pairing of teams in the jousting may have given their team an advantage."

All four of us froze.

"The fact that each team met only one other team in that first round may, in the opinion of the Circle Diamond, have been a source of disappointment to the riders on some of the other teams. Accordingly they have expressed their willingness to meet any riders from any of the teams in a series of extra individual competitions at the conclusion of the grand melee. Any knight who wishes to challenge may name the defending Circle Diamond rider he wishes to engage."

"That's what Karl was doing!" I exclaimed. I explained how, while I'd been waiting to speak to Mr. Brookes, I'd seen Karl come out of the judges' tent.

"What the heck is he thinking of?" Billy moaned. "Is he out of his mind?"

"I guess he's decided he wants us to bleed in earnest for the sake of the good old Circle Diamond," Doug put in.

"He's not official spokesman for the team," I objected.

"No, but he's official spokesman for the ranch."

"Can't your dad go to the officials and explain?"

"He could, but it wouldn't do the ranch much good if everybody decided we were fighting among ourselves."

He was right.

"So, what do we do?" Gus asked.

"Hope very hard that no one will challenge," Doug replied. "Or if they do, that they'll be rotten jousters."

"What a hope."

"Maybe the others won't be any more eager for a replay than we are," I suggested.

"Let's not worry about it now," Doug replied, leading his quarter horse out of the stall. "Let's not even think about it until after we get this grand melee over with. Are you guys ready?"

We followed him to the entrance to the arena where the other teams had already assembled.

We were scheduled to fight against the Double J, the second-place team. When the dancers finished their victory dance, which I couldn't help feeling had been inappropriately named, and the trumpets sounded for the grand melee to begin, Gus, Billy, Doug and I lined up at one end of the open field. The four Double J knights lined up fifty meters away. Then the Grand Knight Marshall dropped his sword as the signal to charge.

The idea was that each knight would wrestle with his opposite number until one was thrown to the ground, then the victor in each pair would swing around and help one of his teammates.

As we charged across the field, Doug's horse was in front with Gus and Billy a close second, while old Brownie wasn't in all that much of a rush. In fact, she wasn't in a hurry at all. As a result Doug had met and thrown his opponent before Brownie and I got into the action.

I saw the Double J knight coming at me. He grabbed my arm. I knew my knee grip wasn't going to be any match for his, so I was studying the ground for what would be the softest landing spot when Doug grabbed him from the other side. Lo and behold, the Double J rider was on the ground and good old Sir Timothy was still mounted! And without so much as a tussle!

Gus and Billy had won their wrestling matches, too, so the Circle Diamond was still in top spot as we rode off the field to the sound of rousing cheers from the spectators.

Then the Flying M knights met the T Bar T, and in that contest the Flying M came out on top.

"Just one more round, Sir Timothy, and we've won the tournament," Doug called out to me as we were assembling at the end of the field, this time to meet the Flying M team.

Again with the drop of the sword the teams charged.

If complacency isn't included among the seven deadly sins, it ought to be. Old Brownie and I should have been humble enough to realize that there is a time and a place for cowardice. We should have proceeded reluctantly, as we'd done before, so Doug, Gus or Billy would have been finished with his opponent and would be free to lend us a hand. But instead of sauntering across the field at a nice, hesitant canter, watching both ways for oncoming traffic that should be given the right of way, old Brownie took off as if she was entered in the Grand National. And instead of immediately pulling her back, I was stupid enough to urge her on even faster. As a result I met my opponent at exactly the same second as Doug and Gus and Billy met theirs.

There's a law in physics that says matter inside a vehicle continues to travel at the same rate after the vehicle stops. That's why we're supposed to wear seat belts in cars and airplanes. But apparently no one has ever thought it worthwhile to apply that principle to horses.

Brownie was setting a track record across the

field. When the Flying M knight appeared in front of us, arms outstretched, Brownie put on the brakes. Obeying that law of physics, I kept traveling at the same rate. Without a seat belt the only thing I had working for me was my knee grip, which wasn't all that great.

Mind you, under ordinary circumstances I'd have been all right if I'd braced my feet hard and broken the cardinal rule of horsemanship by grabbing the horn. Then I might have managed to stay on board. But I couldn't grab the horn. Not because I had any guilt feelings about violating the code, but because I couldn't get my hands on it. My opponent had hooked me under the armpit and my arm was all tangled up in his. The next thing I knew I was on the ground.

It wasn't like the falls I'd taken in the jousting bouts. In the first place, there wasn't any nice soft sawdust. In the second, there's a right way and a wrong way to fall off a galloping horse, and the right way isn't with your leg twisted under you.

I heard the snap, and it made me feel sick. Then the pain started and I didn't have time to think about feeling sick.

What happened after that is a little hazy. I know Doug and Gus and Billy threw their opponents and wrestled down the Flying M knight who had thrown me, because Mr. Brookes told me so as he was driving me to Kamloops to get my leg set. But it wasn't until late the following afternoon that I heard what finally happened in the tournament.

The doctor had said it was okay for me to leave the hospital and go back to the ranch as long as I stayed really still for forty-eight hours while the plaster set. I promised him I would. Now I was back in my room, propped up in bed, with my leg encased in plaster right to the hip.

Just before dinnertime Hilary and Doug came up to see how I was doing.

"We sure miss your strong right arm with those irrigation pipes," Doug said, tossing his sweat-stained Stetson onto the floor and sinking into the armchair by the window. Apparently he and Gus and Billy had been working like mad all day trying to catch up on some of the jobs that had been allowed to slip while we'd been playing knights.

I grinned. It probably wasn't true, but it was nice of him to say it. Then I remembered. Ever since yesterday afternoon, when I'd done my Russian Cossack imitation, I'd been feeling too rotten to think about anything but pain, but during the last little while my mind had started working again.

"What did your dad say to Gus and Billy when they went to see him yesterday after the tournament?" I asked. "Did he tell them it was okay? Are they off the hook?"

"He was too busy taking you to the hospital to talk to anybody," Doug said wryly. "But he talked to them this morning. First of all, he apologized for not having believed them, then he wanted to know why they hadn't proved they weren't in the barn by coming out and saying where they were."

I raised my eyes skyward. "And?"

Doug smiled. "I guess your example must have rubbed off. They owned up, too."

"About the beer?"

"Uh-huh."

The word was noncommittal. It was impossible to guess what Doug was thinking, but I had an awful sense of premonition. "Did your dad get mad all over again?"

"Gus and Billy thought he was going to. Apparently he looked pretty stern and reminded them of the ranch's rules about that sort of thing during working hours. But he couldn't have been too mad because all he said was not to do it again."

I was so relieved I pushed myself upright, forgetting about my leg.

I wouldn't forget again. When the pain had subsided enough for me to speak, I asked weakly, "What about the challenge jousts? Did you go through with them?"

As I was speaking Mr. Brookes appeared in the bedroom doorway. He answered before Doug could. "I didn't want them to. As soon as I realized that you'd been hurt I went to the officials and explained that there were only three riders left and asked them to announce that the Circle Diamond would be forced to take back its challenge offer. The announcer had just called for attention over the public address system when Doug came running over. He insisted that all three of them wanted to go ahead with the challenges."

"Why?" I asked, stunned.

Doug was grinning from ear to ear. "It was the only way we could prove once and for all that the Circle Diamond was unquestionably the best team and hadn't just won by a fluke. Besides, we knew all twelve riders wouldn't challenge."

"How many did?"

"Eight. Four said they wanted to fight Gus, three picked Billy and one challenged me."

"Makes sense. They knew you'd be the toughest to beat."

Doug tried to protest but nobody paid any attention, for we all knew he'd been top scorer in the tournament.

"I think Karl may have had something to do with it," Mr. Brookes suggested. "I think he planted the idea in some of the challengers' minds that Gus and Billy were the ones who should be tested."

"How did you make out?" I prodded, dying with curiosity.

Again it was Mr. Brookes who answered. "Right on top. They lost a couple of contests and two were a draw. But the other four they won. I don't think anyone at the rodeo has the slightest doubt that our jousting team was best in the tournament."

Doug was beaming.

I was as delighted as he was. I leaned back against the pillows and closed my eyes.

But Doug must have stopped beaming, because suddenly, in a voice that didn't have any lightness at all in it, he asked, "Will Karl stop picking on Gus and Billy now?"

I opened my eyes and straightened up again, only carefully this time.

For a moment there was silence. I saw Doug's face tighten as he watched his dad.

Some flecks of dust on Mr. Brookes's jacket seemed to be requiring his attention. "I passed along Tim's message, as I'd said I would yesterday morning," he said at last in an overly careful tone, "but Karl was pretty busy with one thing and another and we didn't have time to talk. I knew he'd be catching the closing events at the rodeo in the afternoon, so after Tim was settled in the hospital I went back to Falkland and found him. I told him that as far as I was concerned we'd all done some hasty things and had made some mistakes. I suggested that we should forget everything that had happened during the past couple of weeks and go back to the way things were before the Gambler incident, but he said he wasn't willing to go on working with Gus and Billy any longer."

I was watching Doug. All the life had drained out of his face. "And you went along with that?"

"I had no choice. He was my foreman, after all. He had a right to speak his mind. He made it clear I had to choose between him and Gus and Billy."

Doug had risen from the chair he'd been sitting in. Now he turned away and stared out the window. It reminded me of that day just over a week ago when I'd stood at the same window and listened while Karl had blasted Gus and Billy about the baler twine.

Mr. Brookes was no longer studying his jacket sleeve. "I've given the matter a lot of thought over the past twenty-four hours, Doug." His voice was firm. "Karl is an outstanding foreman. He has run this ranch for me for eight years, and during that time every operation has been geared to mesh perfectly with every other one."

There was a pause. I could tell from the way the muscles across Doug's shoulders had tightened that he was clenching his fists.

"Do you think you'll be able to develop that knack?"

Doug turned from the window. The expression

on his face was a funny mixture of hope and disbelief.

"As I told you, Karl made it perfectly plain that I had to make a choice — either him or Gus and Billy. So I've got a job open for a new foreman. Like to give it a try?"

Doug's face was like a three-year-old's at a magician's show. "You mean that, Dad?"

"Why not? You'll soon be nineteen. I was only a few years older than that when I started to run this place."

"And you're not going to fire Gus and Billy?"

"How can I? I remember my new foreman telling me once that they were the best workers on the ranch."

I was watching the expressions on Doug's face as Mr. Brookes had been talking. They had run the full range from anger through puzzlement, to disbelief and finally to excitement.

For a moment Mr. Brookes continued to smile at Doug, then he looked at me. "Well, that pretty well takes care of Doug and Gus and Billy. Now what about you, Tim? When your folks sent you here, they didn't expect you to end up like this. Would you like me to arrange to fly you home as soon as the doctor says you're fit to travel?"

I stole a quick glance at Hilary. All this time she'd been sitting quietly, just listening, but the way she was looking at me told me everything I needed to know. "If you wouldn't mind putting up with me for a while longer, Mr. Brookes," I said self-consciously, "I'd kind of like to hang around till the end of the summer." I looked down at my plaster leg. "I guess I won't be good for much, but maybe I could lend a hand in the kitchen or something — peeling potatoes, maybe."

"You'd better get some lessons before you volunteer," Doug suggested, still grinning like a three-year-old. "With your track record, it could save the ranch a fortune in bandages."

I smiled back at him, but before I could come up with a reply, the call came from downstairs that dinner was ready.

Mr. Brookes and Doug got to their feet.

As Doug followed his dad out the door I heard him asking if it would be okay to tell Gus and Billy about his being the new foreman.

"By all means," Mr. Brookes replied.

I glanced at Hilary. She was still sitting in the corner, still watching me with that same expression in her eyes.

"Hi," I said, because I couldn't think of anything else.

"Hi," she answered.

Then there was silence. I had to say something. "Aren't you going for dinner?" I managed.

Her eyes crinkled up and I knew she was laughing at me. "Right this minute, but I'll be back with yours, Sir Lancelot."

She got to her feet. Then before I realized what was happening she leaned over the bed and kissed me. Not a quick peck on the cheek the way she'd kissed Doug on Saturday morning, but slowly and properly — right on the mouth.

Then she was gone.

I lay back against the pillows and stared at the white ceiling, which I'd come to know pretty well these past few weeks. I thought back to the first day when I'd stretched out on the bed and stared at it.

All in all, it was turning out to be a pretty good summer.